The Greek Constellations -
Cancer and Leo

The Greek Constellations - Cancer and Leo

Stephan De Jonghe

Contents

iii

Copyright

For permission requests, write to the publisher at: stephansfolliclefarm@gmail.com

Ordering Information:
Special discounts are available on quantity purchases by book resellers, corporations, associations, and others. For details, contact the publisher at the email address above.

The Greek Constellations – Cancer and Leo - Second edition by Stephan De Jonghe

ISBN 978-0-6453718-8-8 (paperback)
ISBN 978-0-6453718-9-5 (e-book)

Publisher
Stephan De Jonghe Publishing,
Hillarys, Perth, Western Australia, Australia 6025

Printer and distributor
Ingram Content Group
1 Ingram Blvd.
La Vergne, Tennessee USA 37086

The dedication

The dedication.

To say that my darling wife is the love of my life
is an understatement.

Deb is my best friend, soul mate, confidant, and life partner.

Among so many other things, we also share a love of books, and we have
a massive library on display in our home of books that we want to read.

Our topics include action, comedy, romance, science fiction, crime,
thrillers, and adventure.
We also have an impressive non-fiction collection.

My endeavours as an author represent a passion that
burns powerfully for me. I am driven to write.

I have many stories to tell and writing them and publishing them is my
way of contributing to other people's library's.

Writing involves many hours of research and then sitting in solitude,
slowly assembling the words that details a journey into a readable story.
One that was only previously an idea.

This takes a lot of patience and persistence.
After the story is put down, the process of editing begins.

Few non-writers understand that this stage can take as much five times longer than it takes to write the actual first draft.

My Deb gives me the support that I need to execute my writing passion. She not only supports my writing, but also enjoys reading the stories.

Her assistance with proof reading, feed-back on content, and editing, is invaluable.
Especially after I have become blind to my own errors.
She understands how important it is to me and to you, the reader, to get it right.

I dedicate these books to my wife as my thanks to her for her ongoing support, and for her contributions to the finished publications.

We are a team.

We both hope that you enjoy this series of books, and we look forward to your feedback.

Stephan and Deb De Jonghe

Special Thanks

My special thanks go to Janey Emery – Renowned Australian artist, for giving me permission to use her art for the covers for my Greek Constellation series of books.

"I hope you enjoy her art and the story within these pages."
Stephan De Jonghe - Author

Janey's Story - Born in Narrogin, Western Australia, Janey Emery's interest in art began as early as 2 years of age and led to art becoming the central element in Janey's Childhood. Excelling in art throughout her school years Janey devoted herself to the art course provided by Balcatta Senior High school, where her passion for art only intensified.

Janey has been painting fulltime since 1991 and has attained a high degree of respect in the art world from peers and art lovers alike. Janey has won numerous distinguished artistic awards for her work and has sold many paintings throughout Australia and overseas. Janey Emery is achieving the recognition her distinctive artistic talents deserve.

Janey is Self-Taught in All Mediums with the exception of leisure courses undertaken in oil and water colours.

"Art has always played a part of who I am. From early childhood to now there has been a need for me to express myself through drawing and painting. I find peace in my craft, and I hope I bring that to my paintings."

"To me, my Art is like breathing. Painting is my life."
Janey Emery - Artist
https://www.janeyemery.art/

A note from the Author

Author's note: Many thousands of years ago, the origins of the constellations Leo and Cancer were two of the many stories imagined by ancient travelers and sailors. In this story I've also included the story behind the constellations "The Hydra" that Herakles defeated during his second labour, "Aquila" or The Eagle which was killed by Herakles during his rescue of Prometheus, "Sagitta" or "The arrow" which is a star cluster in honour of the arrows used by Herakles to kill that eagle, and "Herakles" the constellation that Zeus created to honour the Greek hero!'

This story is based on Greek mythology. "Leo" is the Latin word for Lion, and "Cancer" is the Latin word for Crab. The legends behind both these star signs are entwined. The accounts of the birth and life of Herakles are relevant to both stories and so I have chosen to portray the account of Leo and Cancer together in order to achieve continuity.

Many of these stories owe some of their earlier history to the Phoenicians, Babylonians, and Mycenaean's, and were initially used to help ancient travelers remember star patterns as a nighttime navigational tool. Over time, these fascinating stories were greatly embellished on how the constellations came to be formed. The ancient Greeks called these constellations the "Katasterismoi" meaning, "the placing of the stars." They gave names and told stories about forty-eight out of the eighty-eight constellations that are recognised by the International Astronomical Union.

These mythologies were embellished as they were countlessly re-told with tales of gods encountering wild creatures, fighting fierce battles, and of course having lots of sex. After all, these men were away from home for lengthy periods of time. They shared these stories to entertain urban dwellers that they encountered, and from there the stories became legends, and for many people they became their religion.

A Greek poet and storyteller named Homer, was the first person to document these stories and he is most famous for the "Iliad" and the "Odyssey" which he composed some 2,800 years ago. Whilst very little is known about Homer, he is regarded by many as the founder of modern literature. His two main works were the first literary works to be taught formally to students. Interestingly, there are thirty-three film adaptations of the Odyssey, proving his works are still relevant to modern audiences.

Later, a poet named Hesiod, significantly contributed to Greek mythology and followed on from Homer's work. Together they are attributed with establishing ancient Greek religious customs, formal astronomy, the development of structured learning, documenting events, early economics, commercial farming, and time keeping.

The word "zodiac" originated from the Greek words "Zodiakos kuklos," meaning "circle of little animals". It wasn't until 50BCE that the first classical zodiac depicting the twelve astrological star signs in their current order was first depicted. It is known as the "Dendera zodiac."

During the 2nd century CE, a Greco-Roman astrologer and astronomer named Claudius Ptolemy worked on his documented Tetrabiblos into what is regarded as western astrology's primary source document and remains largely in use today. Also of note is that astronomers have named a crater on the Luna surface, and another on the surface of the planet Mars Ptolemaeus, in honour of Ptolemy and his contribution to astronomy.

The connection between Greek names and Roman names for the same deities came from their translation from one language to the other. In ancient Greek, Zeus is pronounced Dias. In Latin that became Djous Pater (Sky *father) or Luppiter. In English this became Jupiter. Many names evolved in this way.*

As an author, my goal is to turn what is known of the mythology, into an enjoyable story for today's reader.

Stephan J De Jonghe

Chronology

Chronology – Yet another note from the author, Stephan De Jonghe

My "from astronomy to mythology" series of novellas posed some difficulties in terms of writing the stories into a logical chronology. Until the Iliad, and the Odessey, no one had ever written any of the tales of titan's forming the world, or their ultimate defeat by the gods who eventually resided in Mount Olympus. These stories were imagined piecemeal, embellished, refined, and retold over a thousand-year period. Unlike history, which did happen on a linear timeline and can be plotted, the timeline used in fictional stories were not relevant, and by their very nature at the whim of the storyteller. Over the millennia, re-tellers of the stories frequently added details, and characters that were often inconsistent with the other stories. No one knew and no one cared, as they were mostly just for entertainment.

For the more serious devotees, these stories were the basis for a religion, and many aspects of the stories were used to focus worshippers' attention, and they were therefore treated by many at the time as historical facts. They focused their attention on those gods and goddesses that were consistent with their beliefs and values.

The best example that I can use to demonstrate the challenge of chronology, is referencing a main character known as Pandora. As she is the first human woman, she features in her own story, but she was created by Hephaestus, the son of Zeus and Hera, and it happened when Zeus and Hera were already married. But Zeus met and fell in love with Europa, a human woman, who was alive before he married

Hera, and before he had a son to ask to make the first woman. Challenging!

As an author with a particular attention to detail, (at least I believe I do), the chronology of Greek mythological events became increasing important to me as the list of novellas planned for this series grew to thirteen.

I have therefore prepared a simple chronology (that may or may not be consistent with other writers of this genre) to assist readers in sorting out the sequence of events that occur in the stories that I am sharing with you. (Spoiler alert!)

I now believe that Greek Mythology Chronology should be a legitimised field of study all on its own. (Perhaps it already is?)

The novella.	The details of the event.
Pisces	Gaia forms the earth, oceans and skies. She is the earth mother.
Pisces	Gaia gives birth to Uranus.
Pisces	Cronus is born and defeats Uranus when he is released from confinement.
Pisces	Aphrodite is born.
Capricorn	Pricus is the father of the sea-goats.
Pisces	Cronus is crowned king and marries Rea. Zeus is one of their six children.
Centaurus	Cronus mates with Philyra. Chiron is born.
Pandora	Prometheus creates a race of human men - It is known as the golden age.
Pisces	Zeus defeats Cronus and Zeus is crowned King of the Gods.
Pisces	Zeus marries Metis, Athena is born, but Metis dies.

Pandora	Prometheus creates a second race of human men - It is known as the silver age.
Pandora	Prometheus creates a third race of human men - It is known as the bronze age.
Pisces	Zeus marries but then quickly divorces Themis.
Pandora	Prometheus creates a fourth race of human men - It is known as the iron age.
Sagittarius	Crotus invents the bow and arrow.
Pisces	Zeus marries Hera. Ares, Eileithyia, Hephaestus, and Hebe are born.
Pisces	Aphrodite arrives at Mount Olympus and marries Hephaestus.
Pandora	Hephaestus creates Pandora as the first human woman.
Taurus	Zeus meets Europa.
Scorpio	Zeus mates with Leto and Apollo and Artemis are born.
Scorpio	Poseidon mates with Euryale and Orion is born.
Scorpio	Atalanta is recused as an infant and she now runs with Artemis
Aries	Zeus creates a cloud nymph named Nephele.
Aries	Poseidon mates with Theophane and Chrysomallos is born.
Aries	Nephele marries Athamas and Helle and Phrixus are born.
Aries	Chrysomallos rescues Helle and Phrixus.
Ophiuchus	Apollo mates with Coronis and Asclepius is born.
Cancer/Leo	Zeus mates with Alkmene and Herakles is born.
Gemini	Zeus mates with Leda and Polydeuces and Castor are born.
Pisces	Aphrodite mates with Ares. Eros is born.

Scorpio	Orion meets and befriends Hephaistos.
Virgo/Libra	Zeus visits Themis and Astraea.
Cancer/Leo	Herakles is assigned the first of his ten labours.
Cancer/Leo	Herakles befriends Chiron.
Centaurus	Chiron befriends Herakles.
Gemini	Castor and Polydeuces join the Argo crew
Cancer/Leo	Herakles joins Argo crew.
Gemini	Atalanta asks to join Argo crew.
Scorpio	Orion meets Artemis.
Centaurus	Chiron commences as a teacher.
Gemini	Herakles is inadvertently separated from the Argo.
Cancer/Leo	Herakles resumes his labours.
Scorpio	Orion duels with the giant scorpion.
Gemini	Jason and Argo crew return with the Golden Fleece.
Gemini	Calydonian Boar Hunt.
Gemini	Atalanta joins the Calydonian Boar Hunt
Cancer/Leo	Herakles accidentally wounds Chiron
Centaurus	Chiron makes his plea to Zeus.
Pisces	The Greeks and the Trojans start a war that lasts ten years.
Aquarius	Zeus meets Ganymede.
Cancer/Leo	Herakles becomes immortal and marries Hebe.
Pisces	Atalanta competes in a running race against her potential suitors.
Gemini	Castor and Polydeuces become immortal.
Pisces	Aphrodite an Eros escape Typhon.

The story of Cancer and Leo

Zeus's home was a palace that was situated high up on the slopes of Mount Olympus. From there he ruled over all the gods and goddesses who attended to humanity. As Zeus's rested alone in his bed chamber, far from the maddening demands of his regal duties, a servant begged his lord's attention. 'Master!' he said in hushed tones, but he still managed to convey some urgency in his voice. Everyone knew that the risk of choosing to disturb this god came with some personal risks.

'Hmm,' murmured, Zeus. He slowly opened his eyes as he awakened from a peaceful slumber.

'We've had a report that I thought you might find interesting. We have learned that Amphitryon, King of the Tiryns, is due to return to his home tomorrow after a lengthy campaign. They say, he and his wife Alkmene, are enthusiastic to start a family, so we thought that this will mean that she'll be amorous and passionate when reunited with him.'

'How long was this campaign?' Zeus asked casually, though his interest was piqued. He recalled that Alkmene was a very beautiful woman, and one that he had openly expressed a desire to bed for some time now.

He had trained his staff well. They were delighted to keep him informed about such opportunities. Besides, all of them knew that a satisfied Zeus was much easier to manage that an anxious Zeus.

'Many months, master,' the servant informed Zeus. 'Apparently, he was banned from her bed until he had avenged the deaths of her two brothers'.

'And did he?'

'Yes master, the battle was won. Now he and his army are rejoicing their victory, before they start their long journey home...'

The astonished servant looked about the room, but Zeus was already gone.

***

Zeus enjoyed transforming into a giant eagle. He often did so when travelling his realm and he surveyed the homes and lifestyles of the mortals. As a god he could easily dematerialise and reappear wherever he desired, but flying about in his eagle form always felt satisfying and more productive. From far above, and with his superior eagle eyesight, he saw many opportunities, and that gave him a superior edge over the other less capable terrestrial gods.

As he flew to Tiryn, he thought about the ever desirable, Alkmene. He could not remember all his grandchildren, there were simply too many of them, but this one had always stood out in his memory because of her astonishing beauty. She must have taken after her mother, Andromeda, wasn't it? He wasn't sure. Or perhaps she took after her grandmother, Danaë. He recalled that she was also an especially good-looking woman, and that she was the mother of Alkmene's father, Perseus. Perseus, he was a son to be proud off. As he flew, he reminisced about Danaë. For her, he had turned himself into a shower of gold coins in order to impress her and then seduce her, such fun. She gave birth to Perseus about nine months after his visit. He smirked, recalling that it seemed to have upset her father at the time. So many things had happened since then, it was hard to remember them.

Zeus landed on a tree branch. He hesitated for only a moment as he considered that Perseus might not be all that congenial about his incestuous plans for his daughter. He amused himself thinking about the problem. Since becoming aware that Alkmene had grown into such a lusciously beautiful woman, he had decided that he wanted to have sex with her. Now he felt he had the right opportunity, one that was too good to waste. Besides, his wife Hera was distracted at the moment with her preoccupations of helping other humans. He would simply help himself to one of them. He would disguise himself in such a way that no one would ever know that it was he, who had performed amazing acts of coitus with Alkmene. Zeus now had a plan that he believed would work to mutual satisfaction, so he flapped his enormous wings, flew up higher into the open sky, and resumed his journey.

The trouble with the gods was that they behaved as if they were moralistic when discussing extramarital relationships. You would think that being a god would mean that they would be more liberal, but in terms of illicit liaisons, they tended to be just as indignant about infidelity as humans claimed to be. Zeus was also well aware that most of the gods were bigger hypocrites than their mortal charges.

***

Zeus circled the palace and chose a discreet vantage point to reconnoitre the best approach into the palace. He then landed inconspicuously, and he immediately began watching Alkmene from a distance. She was every bit as magnificent as he had remembered, and he was pleased with himself that he had made the journey to be with her. He also observed frantic activity at the palace where she lived. She was busily ordering servants to complete the preparations for her husband's return. The courtyards were being swept and tidied, festive decorations were being hung, and the palace was being prepared for her husband's triumphant return. Large quantities of fresh vegetables and fruit were being delivered, animals were butchered, and pastries baked all in preparation for the feast and celebrations to come.

Zeus believed Alkmene had done well marrying Amphitryon. He was king of the Tiryns and he was strong, brave, and cared deeply for his people and their wellbeing. He was also loving and devoted to Alkmene. He had worked hard to be a good and benevolent king. Even Hera spoke well of him, which was a rarity, as she considered most husbands to be brainless imbeciles and self-motivated. His only downside was that he was often away from home. It was well known that she missed him terribly, and this made her even more desperate to have his child.

Zeus concluded that she must have felt forsaken during his frequent absences. He pondered about how best to go about bedding her. He needed a clever disguise in order to get away with having sex with her, without anyone knowing that it was him. Then the solution occurred to him. He would disguise himself as Amphitryon. God he was good and it's good to be a god, he thought to himself.

Zeus then transformed himself into a battle weary Amphitryon, and he walked casually out of the dense undergrowth that had afforded him a discreet observation post. He crossed the open area, walked into the front courtyard, and up the stairs to the palace doors. He presented his biggest grin to the assembling crowd, and then waved at everyone. At first, they were all startled, confused, but that quickly changed and became a hero's welcome. They cheered and clapped in appreciation of his return. No one questioned him about his early arrival, nor did they inquire about the whereabouts of his usual retinue of officers and staff. Everyone just assumed that he'd come home ahead of the others, probably to surprise his adoring wife. They all happily cheered, and they applauded their king's return. Zeus was very pleased with himself.

On hearing the commotion, Alkmene rushed into the courtyard, climbed the steps, and leapt straight into his outstretched arms. She kissed and hugged him, and her eyes wept for joy of seeing her husband at last. 'I had hoped that you'd come home early,' she proclaimed.

'I couldn't bear being away from you any longer,' he explained. 'I have missed you so much my darling.'

'Thank you for avenging my brothers,' she whispered into his ear.

As they embraced, the gathering of servants was cheering once more, and were now offering the happy couple positive and adoring compliments. Everyone was pleased that they were once again re-united. He held Alkmene at arm's length to explain a recent decision. 'I have even better news.'

'What is it?' she asked excitedly.

'I'll be staying home for a long time.' He looked deep into her eyes. 'My place is to be here with you'.

She hugged him more tightly than before, if that were possible. She loved him so much and now that she was once more in his arms, she became hungry and passionate for him. Her need to feel him inside of her was becoming urgent. "How long had it been?" she started to wonder but quickly stopped herself. "No, don't think about that, just enjoy this moment."

Alkmene was so happy about her husband's early return that she couldn't stop smiling. Holding his hand, she led him up the stairs to their private chambers. Her bed chamber staff had prepared a bath and she disrobed him, and then guided him to the cleansing waters. She lathered the washcloth with soap and bathed her husband. She delighted upon seeing his erection peek above the soapy water, clearly, he was as excited to see her as she was to see him. She reached down and lovingly fondled it, and he softly groaned in sweet pleasure.

Before Zeus realised what was happening, her clothing had fallen off her gorgeous body and onto the floor. She stepped over the rim, and she was now in the water with him, mounting him whilst he sat in the bath. She was even more beautiful than he could have ever imagined. He was very happy that he decided to come here. It excited him even more that he was being led by her, through all of this exquisite pleasure.

Their successive and deliciously explosive climaxes were both simultaneous and overwhelmingly amazing. And then they both relaxed, their energy depleted, yet both still breathing heavily. The day was drawing to a close and Zeus wondered if he should excuse himself somehow and make his departure under the cover of darkness. Her magnificent breasts were now resting against him, and he could feel her firm nipples press into his chest. He felt the warmth of her naked body nearer to his in the cooling water. He slowly caressed her smooth but firm body, and he could now feel the sensations of becoming aroused once more.

She remained on top of him, and he was still thrust deep inside of her. The bath basin was big, but only just big enough for the two of them. They were again rocking evenly and soon she was moaning once more in sensual arousal. Water from the tub sloshed and soon waves of water spilled over the sides of the bath, as waves of pleasure shuddered through her body once more.

Alkmene quickly recovered. When her energy had sufficiently returned, she dismounted and led him, still wet from the bath water, by his still enormous erect member, directly to the bed. She kissed him passionately on his lips as she caressed his muscular body, and she then smiled as she manoeuvred herself ready to mount him once more.

Zeus looked outside and silently ordered the sun god Helios to "take the following day off". Thus, they would have thirty-six hours of night-time pleasure. Whilst the rest of the world's inhabitants got an extra-long sleep, he and Alkmene would have extra time to copulate. He chuckled to himself, smug with his own ingenuity.

Zeus lost count of the number of times they consummated Alkmene's hunger for her husband. The number of different positions that she wanted him inside of her was impressive, and he wasn't easily impressed. After many hours of passion, they finally slept. It was a bit uncomfortable for him as she insisted that they sleep entwined, and normally Zeus would have preferred not to do that, but given the quality of this experience, he decided he'd just go with it. In the early hours of the morning, he quietly rose to depart but Alkmene stirred beside him. He begged toilet and she fell back to sleep, seemingly agreeable that he'd return soon.

Zeus departed the chamber and hastened away from the palace. He transformed once more into his eagle form and he flew directly to Mount Olympus and his own home. Zeus was naturally conceited enough to think there wouldn't be any consequences to his trickery. He never considered that she'd be confused when her actual husband returned. He didn't care that Amphitryon would not get the reception that he himself had just enjoyed. He was a happy god, a successful god, and at this point in time, he was also a very satisfied god.

"It's good to be me," he told himself as he climbed into his own bed to get some additional sleep.

***

Alkmene awoke to the urgent sounds in the courtyard below her bedchamber window. Looking about her, she realised that she was alone. Her husband was always an early riser, and she assumed that he must now be catching up on the happenings of the palace. She looked out the window and saw his personal guards arriving. They were followed by the many wagons that always travelled with the officers and their clerks who managed her husband's campaigns. She looked for her husband expecting to see him exit the palace to formally greet his men. Some trumpets sounded and then, astride his horse, her husband Amphitryon all sweaty and dusty from his journey home, rode into their courtyard.

Instead of welcoming cheers, the palace staff and other inhabitants of their community only stood still and stared at him in bewilderment. Hadn't Amphitryon already returned home? Wasn't he already inside the palace happily reunited with their queen?

Alkmene was now confused. Had her husband ridden out to meet his men? That did not seem reasonable. She waved to him, and he waved a weary reply. He looked tired and grumpy. She rushed down the stairs to confront him and to try to figure out what was now happening. Alkmene still felt the glow from their night of passionate love making, though she was in some discomfort, and she'd need to rest that part of her body tonight. She had wondered how many times he had entered her, but she was confident that all of his accumulated seed was spent. She flushed with the memory of it. It was so wonderful that he was home and tonight they would talk, and she'd learn more about his successful campaign.

'My darling,' she said as she embraced him when he alighted from his horse.

'It is so pleasurable to see you again Alkmene,' he told her after they'd briefly kissed.

He looked tired. She wasn't surprised because of their lack of sleep last night, but she was confused to see him all dusty and dirty, as if he had just returned from a long journey. 'Why did you ride out to meet your men? Did you think they'd lose their way?' she teased.

'I always ride with my men,' he replied, clearly annoyed at the question. 'A leader leads,' he added.

'Not last night,' she reminded him.

'What do you mean?' he demanded.

'Well,' she smiled. 'Last night, you were delighted to be led.'

'What are you talking about wife?' he demanded, getting agitated with her nonsense.

'Last night,' she reminded him. Her tone was also getting curt. 'When you made love to me for the whole night.' She tried to relax and then she reached up to kiss him, but he pulled away looking annoyed with her.

'You are crazy,' he told her. 'Last night we camped by the river, ate fish and drank too much wine. We celebrated as it was our last day of our journey home.'

'You're the crazy one!' she exclaimed loudly. 'Last night you were in my bed!'

'I'm sure I'd remember something like that,' he smiled as he calmly replied. 'It's all I've been thinking about since we started our journey home.'

'Last night you spent enough seed inside of me to make thousands of babies.'

'I did not,' he replied. 'I may have drunk enough wine to drown a thousand fish. But that was all that was swimming yesterday.' He paused. 'Have you been sleeping with another man?' he asked her calmly a hint of teasing in his voice.

'I only sleep with my husband!' she was now becoming indignant, upset, and confused. Her arms were folded, and tears formed in her eyes. She then doubled over and began to sob.

He tried to hold and comfort her, but she pushed him away. 'There is something wrong here,' he told her evenly. 'Clearly you believe that I came home early and that we made love last night.'

'Yes, we did!' she blurted out through her sobs. 'We made love all night long. I can't believe that you now deny it!'

The other people had looked away, feeling awkward at being present during such a conversation. The palace staff were aware of their night of passion, and they were happy for their mistress.

'But the truth is that last night I was drinking and feasting with my men. They will vouch for it, and I have the hangover to prove it,' he said as he grimaced.

'No! It cannot be so!' more tears.

'We will soon learn the truth. Let me bathe and we'll find some witnesses to last night's events. Nothing is secret or remains private in this place for very long.'

***

Hours later, when Amphitryon was bathed and wearing clean clothing, he found himself eating his meal alone. He ate in silent contemplation of this confusing dilemma. If she had been with another man, then the kingdoms rules dictated that she'd have to be sacrificed, or at least severely punished as a warning to others. She could be executed for both her adultery and her deceit. If her words were the truth however, he'd need to learn the origin of this deception and punish the trickster.

He drank some water and then paced the room. He then went to the servant's quarters and down into the kitchen. His people were now cautious when he approached them. They were confused about his twice returning home from the same campaign. Slowly, he learned from them that he had returned home the previous night. That his wife was overjoyed at his return. One long term trusted servant mustered up the courage to compliment him on his performance. Clearly Alkmene enjoyed her passionate reunion with him, and she was heard by many within the palace expressing that joy. Amphitryon went as pale as freshly washed bed linen. He now realised that Alkmene and all the others, truly believed that it was him that was in bed with his wife on the previous night. He was tired and weary and did not need this. He had been previously hopeful to bed his wife, but now he started to realise that that was not going to happen. It never did when she was angry or upset. He then decided that they would need to consult the prophet and find out what really happened and how.

***

Teiresias was getting old. He could not remember how old he was, but he was sure it was over one hundred. Or perhaps he was only eighty. His eyes were weak. People thought he was blind, but he could still see a little bit. He let them think that he was blind as it helped maintain a degree of reverence and extra care for him. In exchange for the advice that he gave them, the people brought him many gifts of food and drink, as he had little need for money. Mostly, they would share their problems with him, and he would share some clever observations, or make some comforting suggestions in relation to their current plight. They liked to call his responses "prophecies," but he knew it was just mostly common sense. Teiresias was no faker, but he had some skills and the "gift" that had kept him fed, clothed, and sheltered all his life. He liked to joke that he was a Prophet, but not for Profit. Few laughed. Being androgynous meant that he had had few lovers, but that had not bothered him for a least the last ten years or was it thirty. He had few regrets and he still delighted on hearing tales about true love and unbridled passion, when conveyed to him by others.

There was a gentle knock on his door. 'Teiresias!' a voice called loudly.

'I'm blind not deaf!' he replied opening the door.

'My master and his queen beg an audience with you,' the palace servant explained.

'Oh.' A summons from his king so soon after his return surprised him. So much for him being a prophet.

'Are you ready to travel? I have a cart. It is really quite urgent.'

'In that case I'd better come with you straight away. What is the nature of the problem?'

'I'm sorry Teiresias, but I don't know what this is about.'

'Never mind, I'm sure I'll find out soon enough.' He held the man's hand as he aided him onto the cart. They sat in silence as they travelled the dusty road that led to the palace.

***

Alkmene and Amphitryon sat in the audience room in front of Teiresias, who was given plenty of food and wine, and a comfortable chair on which to sit. After the pleasantries were exchanged, the prophet smiled kindly and then asked his inevitable opening question. 'How may I be of service?'

'We seem to have a very unusual problem,' Amphitryon replied. He looked about the room as if seeking some easy inspiration on how to resolve their situation.

'It usually is, my lord,' Teiresias said politely. It was always best to do so with these regal types.

Both Alkmene and Amphitryon calmly shared their account of what happened to them both. Alkmene held back on most of the details of the explicit nature of the intercourse she had previously enjoyed. The old man sat in silence, and without emotion or interruption, took in both sides of their story. They were cordial about it and neither contradicted the other, nor attempted to dominate the account. When they finished, Teiresias noted a welling of tears in the queen's eyes. The kings face remained ashen.

'Please my dear, would you stand up,' Teiresias casually requested of the queen. She looked uncertain, but she stood up as asked, the familiarity and comforting tone he used made it easier for her to cooperate.

'Would you mind coming closer to me as my bones are old, and I'm not as strong as I once was.'

She looked at her husband who nodded his consent, and she stepped nearer to the old man. He then sniffed the air loudly before her and she recoiled. 'We only want the truth...' he looked deep into her eyes and reassured her with his soothing tones. He beckoned her nearer. She stepped closer to him, and he bent forward and gently touched her belly area, as he discreetly sniffed the air once more. 'Thank you. Please, sit back down my dear,' he instructed her.

She sat staring at her husband who managed a weak but reassuring smile. The two waited while the old prophet nodded several times considering his response. He looked at the couple and asked. 'What do you both want to achieve from our meeting?'

'To learn the truth,' Amphitryon replied for both of them.

'The truth may hurt both of you,' warned the prophet. 'Do you both believe that the love you have for each other will survive that hurt?'

'It will!' Alkmene proclaimed. She desperately needed to be believed. She loved her husband, but now, for the first time she also feared him.

'I want it too,' Amphitryon agreed.

'The answer is in many parts,' advised Teiresias. 'Firstly, Alkmene... you were not with your husband on the night in question.'

'What!?' she exclaimed in shock. She looked panicked and as if she considered fleeing the room. He firmly held her arm to comfort her.

'The good news for your husband is that you were deceived, and that you truly believed it was Amphitryon that you took to your bed that night,' he continued.

'Who, how?' Amphitryon demanded angrily.

'You were with Zeus,' he clarified and nodded knowingly. He then continued with his explanation. 'He took your form, Amphitryon, and he then came to your home representing you in all ways. You two have been apart for a long time. Your wife's love and natural longing for you negated any chance of her discovering his deceit.'

Alkmene burst into tears and Amphitryon was at once drawn to provide comfort to her. 'Forgive me, my love,' he asked her gently as they hugged. 'I had cause to doubt, but I am so relieved that I was wrong about you.'

'Secondly,' the prophet continued, 'you are now with his child because of this copulation.' Alkmene burst into tears yet again and her husband held her tightly. Amphitryon said nothing.

'Lastly,' the prophet continued smiling, 'There is still room for one more.'

He released her and they looked at him, puzzled. 'I do not understand,' Amphitryon admitted.

'Only with true love and unrestrained passion, will you be able to give birth to two children. Twin boys will be born. One will be from you, Amphitryon, and the other will be from Zeus's seed. However, you must conceive the second child tonight. If you truly love each other, I feel that this should not pose a problem for either of you?' he asked with a smile in his voice and a twinkle in his eye.

'How will we know who is...' Alkmene was about to ask about parentage.

Teiresias interrupted her with one hand in the air. 'I suggest that it is better that you don't know. Don't you agree?'

They sat silently in contemplation as the couple thought about his advice. After a while, Amphitryon decided to conclude their meeting. 'Thank you, Teiresias. I will see to it that you are handsomely rewarded for your loyalty, service, and words of wisdom. You will be well provided for.'

'It is always my pleasure to be of service to you both, my lord.' He stood and bowed symbolically. 'Naturally, I'll remain totally discreet about what has been discussed here today.' He was pleased that he had remembered to give that assurance.

Amphitryon summoned his staff and gave them instructions to help the old man home, and he then arranged a generous ongoing payment to the kind old man.

As Teiresias journeyed home on the cart, he chuckled to himself. He was glad to have seen Zeus in his eagle form circling the palace grounds.

***

The months leading up to the birth of the twins went quickly and were routine and uneventful. Amphitryon and Alkmene prepared rooms for the two boys in her belly. Their birth was highly anticipated by the people, and the palace staff seemed happy with the prospect of having two children to fuss over and bring joy to the palace.

Zeus's wife Hera however, had learned that her husband had again fathered a child with yet another woman. She was reconciled that she could not control her husband's infidelity, but because she was a spiteful and revengeful wife, she decided she would punish the women, and any of their offspring, for allowing him to copulate with them. Hera sent her daughter Eileithyia to kill both the baby and its mother. Hera knew she did not have the power to control or change her husband's persistent adulterous behaviour, and she did not want to leave him. But she was presently resolved to take out her revenge on any of his offspring.

Eileithyia also had her mother's powers over childbirth. She arrived at the palace disguised as a birthing handmaiden, and then arranged it so she was present during the birth of the twins. After the first small baby boy was born and whisked away to be cleaned, Eileithyia placed a powerful grip on Alkmene's uterus preventing the passage of the second larger baby from entering the world. The pain that Alkmene felt was excruciating, and her other attendants feared the worst. Death during childbirth was a common occurrence, and the birth of twins increased the risk. An experienced handmaiden named Galinthias, spied and recognised the goddess Eileithyia seated before the door. Her arms and legs were crossed, and she was in deep concentration. Galinthias recognised the problem, and in a flash of inspiration she cried out, 'A second son is born!'

Eileithyia instantly leapt up in surprise, thereby releasing her mental hold on Alkmene, and this allowed her second baby to promptly enter the world. Galinthias turned to confront the interloper, pleased with the success of her intervention. But this further angered Eileithyia, who in a burst of rage transformed poor Galinthias into a polecat.

They both quickly exited the palace, Eileithyia to report her failure to her mother, and Galinthias to contemplate her new life as a polecat.

***

The two baby boys looked and sounded healthy. Both Alkmene and Amphitryon were happy and proud parents. They couldn't help themselves, and out of curiosity they examined the babies closely to see if they could tell who the father was. But to their pleasant surprise, they both resembled a baby version of Amphitryon. He radiated with happiness as did Alkmene.

'Do not worry,' he reminded her. 'I said I would love them equally as my own, and I intend to honour that promise.'

'I love you,' she told him, her voice confirming it.

'I love you also,' he replied and he leaned forward to share a kiss with his wife.

'What shall we name them?' she asked him.

'I think we should name this one 'Iphikles,'" he said pointing to the smaller of the two babies. 'And this one we should name, 'Herakles,' he suggested to their mother without explaining why.

'I think these are good names, and I already sense that both of them will make us very proud,' she told him.

***

Hera had previously entered the palace. She was disguised as one of the newly recruited attending servants, and she was now standing in the nursery, choosing to remain in the background. She was still seething about Eileithyia's failure, and so had arranged to be there after his child was born. She could tell just from looking at them which one was Zeus's child. "Fools," she thought to herself, when overhearing the parents' inability to figure out paternity.

She resented Zeus's lust for other women, but knew she was powerless to stop him. If only she did not love him so much, his loose morals would be much easier to live with. As a goddess, Hera was praised for her contribution to woman's fertility. The people often turned to her when they struggled to conceive, but it was so totally different when it was her husband's child, which was being born by another woman. She also strongly advocated the sanctity of marriage, possibly due to the lack of it, in her own turbulent one with Zeus. She had loved him all their lives, first as his sister, and now as his wife. Taking out her frustrations on Zeus's offspring was cold comfort, she knew that. It wasn't as if it was the child's fault. It tormented her that he could do these things with impunity, and so punishing these children, and their mothers, was her way of getting even.

Hera approached the babies and cooed maternally to them. She then picked up Iphikles and smiled lovingly at him, rocking him gently. Returning him to his mother, she next picked up Herakles. Caressing his forehead, and unbeknown to his parents, Hera planted a tumour inside Herakles brain. This was her curse on Herakles, and she knew that under its influence he would do terrible things. She then passed baby Herakles to the adoring king.

'I'll take out the linen to be cleaned,' she announced.

She scooped up the soiled cloths, smiled, curtsied, and left the room. In all the excitement of the twins' arrival, Hera's visit, disguised as a servant, was quickly forgotten.

Before she left the palace grounds, she set in motion a deadly visit to baby Herakles.

***

Several days later, after being bathed and fed, the two baby boys slept soundly in their cribs. Their servants were occupied in other rooms, when two deadly vipers took advantage of their absence to slither into the room via an open window. They quietly approached Herakles bed, and with one snake on either side, they scaled up the bassinet and poised within striking distance of the baby. They looked at each other, flicked tongues, their fangs were already moistened with deadly venom as they arched their necks in readiness to strike. In unison the snakes launched their attack, but baby Herakles caught their necks in his infant hands. He held onto them so tightly, and squeezed the snakes so hard, that within minutes, both snakes were dead. He then casually dropped them to the floor and went back to sleep.

Later that day, a servant checking on the babies found the snakes. At first, she was alarmed, but when she realised that the snakes were dead, she calmed down. She checked on the babies and found that they were both sound asleep. Picking up the snakes by their tails, she threw them out the window, startling a passer-by.

***

In another region of Greece, Typhon, the titan monster of storms, was once again copulating with Echidna, the titan goddess and some-time protector of the grapevine. They were presently in their human bodies, as sex between them could never happen when they were in their monster's form.

Typhon was the deadliest of all the titans. He was the youngest son of Gaia, the titan earth mother. He was huge and could change his shape and size at will. From his head and neck, he could sprout many snake and dragon heads that could accurately project venom and throw flaming bombs. His lower half could transform into viper coils. His body could grow wings strong enough to carry his enor-mous weight, and even in flight, he could fling fire balls from his angry eyes. Typhon's raging breath could uproot trees and destroy buildings. He could generate a storm at sea or on land that was so dev-astatingly powerful that even Poseidon himself could not calm it. Ty-phon was known as the father of the monsters, and even the Gods from Mount Olympus feared him.

Even in her monster form, Echidna was a beautiful nymph from the waist up. But her lower half was that of a very long serpent's tail. She lived mostly in a cave that extended far below ground level. It was only accessible by navigating long thin winding passages that only she could traverse. She would happily appear to engage Typhon in sex, or to trap and eat the flesh of those that she captured, when they ven-tured too close to her burrow. On occasion she would eat the wild goats that invaded the local vineyards and destroyed the plantings. She was therefore mistakenly thought to be a protector of the grapes. Echidna was widely known as the mother of all monsters.

Typhon and Echidna would meet just inside the caves entrance. In their human form, they greedily consummated their lust for each other and together they had produced many off-spring. Each child was feared as monsters, and each were able to take human form whenever they desired.

Now, in their human form, Typhon blew out his cheeks in spent satisfaction of his climax. His smelly breath blew back Echidna's long hair, and she laughed. She too was exhausted. Their copulations often lasted for hours, sometimes even for many days. Inevitably, they would produce yet another child. Echidna could immediately tell when they did, so when she announced to Typhon that 'they had done it again,' he was neither surprised, nor concerned.

'What shall it be this time?' he speculated.

'It is impossible to tell,' she replied laughing. 'Some outrageous beast I should expect, especially when considering its father.'

He laughed and was not offended, as they often teased each other. 'You are a fertile hussy,' he told her with a smile.

'Yes, but I am your hussy,' she reminded him. 'You on the other hand, would copulate with anyone who would have you. So, perhaps you are the hussy.'

'Only for you my dearest, I promise you,' he assured her grimacing in mock pain.

'For now.' Echidna nodded. She knew all about his overwhelming desire to be with Aphrodite.

All her babies were born in their human form. They would gestate quickly, and she usually delivered them within weeks of their conception. Neither Echidna or Typhon considered themselves much as parents, and they were joyously relieved that their little monsters were mostly self-sufficient from birth.

Their offspring included a three headed dog that they had named Cerberus. They sent him to terrorise Hades, but he ended up guarding the gates into the underworld. They had also produced a serpentine dragon and sent him to terrorise the Hesperides, although they later learned that he been recruited by Hera to become their protector and guard dragon.

They also sired a giant Eagle that they sent to live in the snow topped peaks of the Caucasus Mountain region. They later learned that he was ordered by Zeus to eat out Prometheus' liver every day, only for it to grow back during the night, as he was immortal and could not die from his wounds. Prometheus was being punished for giving permission to the humans to use fire to cook meat. He was eventually freed.

Echidna also gave birth to a baby that could change its shape into a nine headed water snake, a Hydra, that they named Astron. His parents decided they would send him to live in the spring swamp named Lake Lerna. Astron was instructed to generally terrorise and eat any of the humans that lived in the area. It turned out that she was both skilled, and overjoyed, with her task.

All their offspring could take human form, but they all preferred to live in their monster bodies.

Three weeks later, Echidna presented her lover with a baby girl. The baby soon surprised them by changing into a snarling, sharp clawed, lion cub, who delighted her parents with her feistiness. Echidna feed her some goat meat that she had left over from a recent kill. Their cub grew rapidly, and she was ready to leave them within weeks of her birth.

'Where shall we send this little monster' Echidna asked Typhon.

'What about, Nemea?' he suggested.

'Why there?' she asked, but he knew she did not really care.

'It has been an uneventful place for the people who live there for some time now. Let us give them a little excitement,' he answered cheekily.

'We'd better give her a name,' she said. 'How about... Zosma?'

So, after a few weeks the young lioness was given a hearty meal and instructions where to go to make a life for herself. With the promise of plenty of plump goats and juicy sheep to eat, the infant lioness set off for Nemea.

If her parents were proud of this child, or any of their brood of monsters, they would never show it.

Soon, they were once more preoccupied with copulating.

***

The young lioness journey was uneventful, and she settled comfortably in her new environs. She hunted, ate, groomed, and slept whenever she wanted.

She smelled her prey long before she had seen it. It was a rabbit. Keeping downwind from the scent, she quietly manoeuvred herself into an attack position. She crouched low and folded down her ears. She examined her quarry, the lay of the land, and calculated the likely route the startled rabbit would take when it became aware of its imminent danger. Her hunger demanded a satisfactory outcome.

The rabbit was fully grown and would make a satisfying meal. Its large ears were constantly rotating, alert to any sounds of danger, and it habitually sniffed the air for the scent of predators. It was grazing on the lush grass near a stream when it somehow sensed danger. Turning towards its burrow, it prepared to hop away to sanctuary, but the lioness was already upon it. The rabbit may have died from fright, or from the jaws ripping through its flesh. Either way, it had made a decent meal and the contented lioness rested briefly before continuing her journey.

***

For Amphitryon and Alkmene, their children's childhood years passed quickly, and they were mostly uneventful. Amphitryon had no longer any desire for battle, and he remained home enjoying a peaceful life with his family. Alkmene cherished him, and she ensured that theirs was that of a happy and contented family. The boys honed their skills of hunting and fighting and all three were formally educated by tutors, disciplined by their father, and wonderfully nurtured by their mother. Iphikles was forever studious, learning languages, arts, and man-management. He was mostly working within the palace doing book work and learning to keep the palace accounts balanced and properly maintained. He had a good head for managing wealth.

As teenagers, Herakles and Iphikles were very different from each other. Herakles readily learnt how to correctly use weapons. He was stronger, and a skilled fighter. He was also a keen student and was good with working the soil to produce crops and raise farm animals. The smaller twin, Iphikles, was better at school learning. He easily learned how to read and write, and he was skilled with numbers. Fortunately, the brothers cared for each other, and they readily helped each other, Herakles with sword and spear skills, and Iphikles with language and counting. Both were gracious in their assistance toward the other.

Even at a young age Herakles could carry heavy things and he often defended his smaller brother from potential bullies and thugs. His brother in turn did most of the talking for the two of them.

Their mother had given birth to their sister, Laonomé three years after the boys, and it was her that Herakles loved to spend his time with. Herakles was always popular with the girls because of his muscular build, which he willingly loved to show off with feats of strength and courage. He carried her everywhere. However, it was Iphikles who was the first to have a steady girlfriend.

Herakles however, preferred to be trained in the arts of battle. He had an appetite for strategy and was good at games. He excelled at learning agriculture, and preferred working outdoors on the farmland and supervising the activities of the farm labourers. All through his childhood, Herakles was plagued by headaches. Some of them were mild, but others could keep him in bed for several days at a time. His parents consulted many physicians, and they were mostly unhelpful. One had prescribed mint tea, and that sort of helped. During those times when the pain was at its worst, he would lock himself in a darkened bedroom, concerned that in his suffering and torment that he might enact harm to others.

Laonomé was kept busy learning the skills that she would need as a future noble's wife, and her brothers saw little of her during the day.

Iphikles was ready for marriage by the time he was nineteen. He had met his future wife when they were just children, and many years earlier she had pledged to one day be his bride. Iphikles loved her, but he had never known anything of love other than the young woman that he was now betrothed too. After their wedding intentions were announced, the family were also told that his future wife was pregnant. No one was surprised, and the prospect of a grandchild seemed to greatly please his parents. Her family had always supported their daughters love for Iphikles, as they believed that as a couple that they were a good match. Their wedding ceremony was a quick, simple, and delightful family affair. Naturally, Herakles was there to support his brother, and he was very happy for them both.

***

The years that passed were also favourable to Zosma. She lived in a cave in the hills near the village of Nemea, which suited her as her den. The cave was littered with the bones of the sheep and cattle that she had killed and eaten. She had often seen groups of human hunters searching for her. She knew that they intended to kill her to stop her from destroying their animals that they seemed to care so much about. The lioness was indifferent to their concerns. She had to eat, and the sheep and cattle that she devoured were easy prey, and they were simply a source of easy food for her.

Then one day, she decided that she would consort with these warriors that persisted in seeking her out. She now wanted to learn more about them. So, the lioness transformed into a woman and dressed herself in clothing that she had painstakingly fashioned from the skins of her kills. She then approached the men and sat nearby, close enough to be seen, but not too close in case she needed to flee. Her lioness instincts dominated her behaviour. The men waved and called to her, but she remained silent and distant. She was surprised that she understood what they were saying, but as she had never spoken words to anyone, or anything in her life, she was not sure if she could.

'Hello,' one man called to her with a wave of his hand.

She waved back.

'Come and join us,' another invited.

'Sit here with me,' a third man suggested patting the ground beside him. They all laughed.

She then realised that they only had friendly and perhaps amorous intentions toward her. She had witnessed mating rituals between humans and between animals and had a fair idea of what went where and why. If only they had known that she was the very predator that they were seeking they might not be so welcoming. She stood up and slowly walked toward them.

'Where do you live?' inquired the biggest man of the group as she came within comfortable talking distance.

'It is far from here,' she told him, surprised to hear her own voice. 'I live several valleys that way with my two brothers.' She pointed to show the direction.

They looked east and then again at her. 'Surely, you have a husband?' another inquired.

'I haven't found the need for having one,' she replied smiling.

They laughed again.

She then learned that her smile seemed to have a wondrous effect on these men. They all seemed in a trance when she spoke, and they sighed when she smiled. She enjoyed this outcome and decided she could use it to her advantage.

'What is your name?' asked the leader.

She hesitated, as she had no idea what her name was. Until then, it had not even occurred to her that she should have a name. Then she thought that her parents must have given her one, but she could not remember what it was. It was not like that there were any other lions living with her for her to talk with.

'What are your names?' she countered, smiling, stalling her response.

'I am Deucalion, and these are my two younger brothers, Glaucas and Catreus.'

'Please tell us your name,' implored Glaucas.

With laughter she invited them, 'Guess my name.'

'Esmeralda, because of your beautiful green eyes?' guessed one.

'No,' she told him.

'She is beautiful,' said another. 'Maybe she is called, Aphrodite.'

The men all laughed loudly at this suggestion. But the lioness did not know who that was, so she just laughed with them. 'I don't think she wants us to know her name,' Deucalion said. He then stood indicating to the others that they should also. 'We must continue our hunt for the lion, and we should return to our camp before it gets too dark.

'I will go home now also,' she told them.

'Please tell us your name!' one man persisted.

The men got up and gathered their weapons and drinking flasks. They headed off in a westerly direction. One man called out to her over his shoulder, 'Goodbye beautiful mysterious woman.'

Only Deucalion lingered. He was statuesque and heavily bearded. He carried a sword and a spear. He studied her intently as if wondering if there was any prospect of being intimate with this woman.

Then suddenly the lioness remembered her name, 'Zosma!' she blurted, pleased with herself. 'My name is Zosma.'

'That is a beautiful name, Zosma. It suits you,' he told her as he walked slowly toward her.

'I'm so relieved that I remembered it. No one calls me by that name, so I forgot,' she explained.

'What do they call you?' Deucalion asked as his curiosity was piqued.

Zosma said nothing, but blushed and looked away.

'I could escort you to your home if you like, Zosma?' he suggested.

'But I live in the opposite direction,' she told him.

'It is no trouble for me, and I'd feel better knowing that you were safely at home with your brothers.'

'I will be fine,' she replied. 'I know these fields and woods intimately and I have no fear of the lion. You must go home to your wife and family.' she advised him.

'Oh, I have none. No wife, or children that I know off,' he added smiling at her, 'I would like to have a wife and a family one day.'

'I am confident that you will soon meet that someone special ...' she countered.

'Maybe... today. I might have done just that,' he intimated as he slowly drew nearer to her.

Zosma laughed with more gusto than she intended, and Deucalion pretended to look hurt.

'Well, maybe you have,' she suggested, her body language was now becoming sexual as she swayed her hips in his direction. His face reacted and he beamed once more with a huge smile. 'Your brothers are going off without you,' she pointed to the two men shrinking in the distance. 'You should hurry, or they will be gone without you.'

He looked in their direction. He turned to her and nodded, as if capitulating to his responsibility to his brothers. 'They are slow,' he assured her. 'I will catch them up easily,' and with that, he turned and headed off to be with the other men.

He then turned to wave his goodbye. 'I hope we meet again, Zosma,' he said.

Zosma waited until he too was gone. She remained in her human form as she headed off to her den. She soon discovered that she was being followed. Crouching behind some boulders she easily spotted him. It was Deucalion, the tall, bearded man that had lingered and had spoken with her just before.

'This human is persistent,' she said to herself. 'I wonder if all human males are like this.'

The man was in a hurry, and he almost walked past her.

'Looking for me,' she called to him.

'Yes,' he said in a puffed-out voice. 'I was concerned for you.'

'That's very sweet of you,' she replied smiling at him.

He dropped his weapons and then came toward her with his arms extended. As soon as he was near, she let her clothes fall to the ground. He gasped, startled by her nakedness. She then morphed into her lioness form and killed him instantly with her first strike of her paw, her fully extended razor-sharp claws easily ripping through the flesh on his face and neck. His blood spurted violently from multiple wounds as he convulsed and rapidly bled out.

The lioness stood over her fresh kill. 'I have never eaten human before,' she thought to herself then sniffed the air, the smell of blood and raw meat increasing her appetite. 'There's a first time for everything.'

***

Despite his headaches, Herakles was mostly a happy man. He had fallen in love and married a beautiful young woman named Magara, and they were very happy together. She gave birth to two healthy sons, and they were named Orpheus and Sisyphus. Orpheus was nearly thirteen and Sisyphus was already fifteen. They both idolised their father, and they especially loved it when he took them on adventures, and when he trained with them to improve their fighting and hunting skills. There cousin, Iolaus was often with them, and together the three learned weapon use, and agriculture and farm animal management, from Herakles.

At thirty-eight years of age, Herakles was more confident, faster, stronger, and more physically skilled than his twin brother, Iphikles. But, because of Herakles persistent headaches, it was decided by their parents that Iphikles alone would inherit the kingdom from their father.

Herakles bore him no grudges. Even though they had grown up as equals in the eyes of their parents, he conceded that he would make a poor king and that the people would be better served under Iphikles leadership. Besides, he was restless and wanted to explore the country and learn more about other peoples.

Herakles parents still believed that he had become a great leader, and so they sent him to Chiron for advanced training and tuition. They also hoped that the Centaur could help him with his headaches. Many months later, when Herakles returned home, wiser, and more skilled, sadly his plague of headaches remained.

Herakles was master of the crops. He introduced irrigation to his father's lands and had streams dammed and coverlets constructed for that purpose. He supervised the harvest of bumper crops and was celebrated for it. He also was quick to lead the men into battle during the defence of the kingdom from marauding tribesmen. His skills with the sword, bow and arrow and spear, became legendary. His only downside was his continuing blinding headaches.

'What is wrong, my darling,' asked Magara all concerned. She already knew the symptoms.

'It's coming again,' he told her.

Magara looked down as if searching for the right words. Herakles was in pain again, and she was frustrated, not knowing how to help the man she loved.

'Maybe you should lie down and rest,' she recommended him.

'Maybe, I should slit my own throat,' he replied evenly.

Magara had heard this type of talk before, and she knew when to be quiet and let her husband deal with it on his own. Herakles sat at the table with his head cradled in his huge hands when his sons burst into the room. They were brandishing practice swords and Orpheus had retreated and was now seeking the protection of their mother, but Sisyphus had pursued him, and they continued their sword play indoors. This was strictly forbidden.

Magara calmly asked the children to stop and be calm, but Orpheus on seeing his brother relax his defences, took the opportunity to gently poke his brother in the chest.

With wounded pride and a small mark on his chest, Sisyphus screamed in exaggerated pain and indignation.

Herakles's headache was at its worst. He screamed in outrage toward his family, stopping them all in a frozen stance. He held out his hand toward the boys in a demand that his son's surrender their swords. They did so and he was making ready to snap them in two when Magara defended her boys.

'They were just playing!' she exclaimed. Please do not break their swords. They just want to be warriors like you!' she added.

Herakles hesitated and then drew a deep breath, he visibly relaxed, and did his best to calmly explain. 'My headache is worse today boys. Please, go outside to play.'

The boys at once obeyed. They had seen their father in pain before, and they knew to leave him alone.

'I will try to sleep this off,' he told his wife. 'I'll give these back to the boys when I'm feeling better,' he explained as he held up the swords confiscated from the boys.

She then gave him the look.

He capitulated. 'I'll even play with them for a while.'

She hugged him lovingly and then Herakles went into their sleeping chamber. Magara followed behind him and drew the curtains as she knew that he would prefer the dark, and he needed peace and quiet to minimize his pain.

'Could you please make the mint broth for me?' he asked of her. 'It seems to help.'

'Of course,' she told him, but then remembered. 'But we have none left, so I will send the boys to get some more from the palace gardens.'

'There are times, when I believe that I can't cope with this any longer,' he told her.

'You have us to care for you, my love.'

'I'm a very lucky man,' he replied.

She left the room, closing the door gently behind her.

Herakles rested but could not sleep. He examined the swords in the near darkness. They were a good length and had a good balance. They were a bit sharp for practice swords. He concluded that the boys must have sharpened them. He decided he would blunt them down before returning them to the boys. He swung one of the swords playfully through the air, but a stab of pain in his head reminded him that he needed to rest. Still clutching the swords grip, he rolled onto his side facing the wall and fell into a deep dreamless sleep.

Magara had sent her sons to the palace kitchen gardens to ask for the mint she needed to make a soothing broth for her husband. The boys were spotted by their grandmother, Alkmene. 'What are you doing boys?' she asked them.

'Grandma,' they yelled in unison as they rushed up to greet her.

After a hug, they informed her of their father's plight. 'Father is sick again.'

'Oh dear,' responded Alkmene. 'These headaches seem to be becoming more severe and more frequent.'

'Mother asked us to fetch mint for father's broth,' Sisyphus explained.

'I will help you gather it, and we will go to your home together. I would like to check up on my son.'

'He is sleeping,' Orpheus informed her.

'Well then, we will have to be very quiet,' assured Alkmene, whispering conspiratorially, and the boys laughed. The brothers, accompanied by their grandmother Alkmene, chattered as they walked the short distance to Herakles home.

'Mother,' Magara exclaimed as she saw her mother-in-law when they finally arrived. 'I am so glad you are here,' she told her. 'He is suffering from a very bad one.'

'I wish we knew the cause of it,' replied Alkmene.

'This broth should help,' said Magara adding the mint leaves to the pot of boiling water she had prepared. They talked quietly until the broth was ready. Magara scooped out a serving into a clay pot, and then quietly entered their bed chamber. 'Herakles, I have your broth,' she told him gently.

Herakles said nothing. 'Herakles!' Magara persisted, but still there was no response.

Concerned for her husband's wellbeing, she rolled him towards her. Herakles, startled from being awakened from his deep sleep, believed he was being attacked. With the boy's sword still in his hand, he lashed out at his assailant, and slit the throat of his attacker. Magara fell to the ground. She was dead before she hit the floor. Realising that it was his wife that he had just killed, he screamed at the horror of what he had done, just as the boys rushed into the room. Herakles saw the horrified look on his son's faces and so he did not hesitate. He decided there and then that they should all die. He would end their lives, as well as his own on that day, rather than live with the consequences of killing their mother and the woman he loved so deeply. With a single sweep of his arm, both boys' necks were slashed with the sword. They both fell to the floor bleeding profusely. He then turned the point of the sword onto his chest, fully intending to take his own life, when his mother raced into the room. 'Stop!' Alkmene screamed and Herakles hesitated. On seeing his mother, he burst into tears and the sword fell to the ground. She kicked away the sword and then reached down and held her son as he broke down in chronic agony. Other women rushed into the room and saw to the boys. Their injuries were potentially fatal.

Alkmene screamed at her son for his violent actions. She moaned and wept about the life-threatening injuries to her grandsons, and for the tragic death of her beloved daughter in law.

***

The lioness was now meticulously grooming herself after feasting on a freshly killed bull. The enormous beast was a challenge for her to drag into her den, and she was gratified that she had been able to do it. She surveyed her home. She had thought to change into human form and tidy up the piles of bones that littered the cave. She had not yet done so as they were her trophies and a source of personal pride. She now had a neat pile of human skulls that she was particularly proud of. She mused that Hades, God of the underworld, would be proud of her. The cattle and sheep she ate were to satisfy her hunger, and she only killed the human hunters in self-defence. She ate them also, as she did not like to waste food, but they were not as tasty as the domestic animals.

She had spent time observing the humans attending their sheep and cattle. She left them to it and only hunted in unattended pastures and took the tastiest looking beasts. Mostly, she killed under the cover of darkness. It was then that the prey was docile and easy to catch, and the humans were away, presumably asleep. She would single out several of the animals and drive them toward her den, so that she would have the cover of the trees when she dragged her kill home to eat.

When humans were hunting her, they were noisy and smelly. Their scent proceeded them, and so it was easy to keep downwind of their approach. A few times, for a bit of fun, she had transformed into a naked woman, pleading for their help. She had learned that they were ever too pleased to do this and would willingly drop their weapons in their haste to comfort her. She would feel their desire for her as their eyes ravished her body. Her long, lean, and perfectly formed naked body, with her long mane of golden hair, and her desperate pleas for their aid was enough to weaken any man. They would rush to her side and try to comfort her, just as she would change back into her lioness form and savage their bodies with her bared teeth and extended claws.

Lately, she had thoughts that it might be nice to allow one of the men to consummate their lust for her. Then she would kill and eat him. She was getting older and thought it might now be nice to produce some lion cubs to keep her company, and to teach them how to share in the fun of the hunt.

***

Herakles deeply grieved for the death of his wife and sons. He hated himself for their slayings, and he laboured continuously in the fields with plough and worked long hours with the livestock. His family could see that he was punishing himself, and they gave him a wide berth for him to work through his private agony.

Even though his two sons were slowly recovering from their wounds, Herakles was not told of this. It was agreed that until Herakles fate was decided, he would not know about their condition. To give him hope in the face of a probable death penalty seemed cruel, so they decided to wait until his sentence was announced before they shared news of the boy's recovery with him.

'If only Teiresias were still alive,' commented Amphitryon to his wife. 'He would have known how to help our son.'

At the inquest, Herakles was partially forgiven his crimes as they had concluded that he was mentally unaware of his actions at the time. The court ruling was that he needed specialised help to cure his headaches. He was ordered to be sent away from Tiryn and seek out either medical or spiritual help for his condition. They told him to seek out the oracle in Delphi. Furthermore, he was banished from Tiryn and ordered to never return.

Herakles had acknowledged the judgment without comment. He looked pale.

'It is better that he believes his sons are dead, as it'll make his banishment easier for him to accept,' Amphitryon commented to his wife.

She stared at him, but then capitulated and nodded her agreement.

The following day he hugged his parents, sister Laonomé, brother Iphikles, sister-in-law, and his nephew Iolaus, and left his family home, agreeing never to return.   A crowd of friends were there to wave him off. They had offered gifts of food and drink for the journey, but Herakles, though touched by their gestures of concern, preferred to travel light.

'May I walk with Uncle?' Iolaus asked his father, Iphikles.

'For a short while,' Iphikles answered.

Iolaus chased after Herakles shouting 'Uncle, Uncle! Wait for me.' Herakles turned as Iolaus ran up to him. 'I will walk some of the way with you, Uncle,' he told him.

At eighteen years of age Iolaus was more like his uncle than his father. He was skilled with weaponry and clearly had an aptitude for outdoor work. He had no ambition to be an administrator or a politician like his father.

'When I'm older, I want to be like you,' he told is uncle.

'I thought you already were!' laughed Herakles.

'May I find you one day and join you on your travels?' asked Iolaus earnestly.

'With your parents' consent, I'd be proud to travel with you as my companion.'

Iolaus whooped in delight.

As they walked, Herakles and Iolaus talked about imagined future adventures, but after a few hours, Herakles sent him home. It was a sad separation for both of them.

His journey to Delphi was mostly uneventful. When other travellers came upon this huge man, they saw a warrior laden with a backpack of food and clothing and heavily armed with bow, arrows, sword, knives, axe, and a long spear. They could not see the madness that he was burdened with or feel his anguish. None the less, they gave him plenty of room and showed him every courtesy.

***

After a five-day journey, Herakles arrived at Delphi. He approached an important looking city official, who was dressed in fine clothing, and was attended too by a man servant. 'Sir,' he started his question, trying his best to sound polite and respectful. 'Could you please direct me to the Oracle?

The man looked at the asker and assessed the giant before him. He was a big man and heavily armed. His clothes, though dirty, were of a good quality. His manners were respectful. He decided he would co-operate with some modest reservation. 'Why do you seek the Oracle?' he asked.

'I have a madness that I hope will be cured by the Oracle,' Herakles told him and then winked.

The official made a quick determination. The Oracle may be able to help a person with madness. Also, this giant of a man wandering the streets could pose a danger to others. Whilst everything was still in order, it may be better to assist this one to avoid making a currently safe situation, escalate into a potentially dangerous one.

A woman approached. She was tall, impressively dressed, and she had an armed escort. 'I know this man, councillor,' she informed the city official.

'He claims to have madness and requires the services of the Oracle,' he informed her.

'I know, and I will make it my responsibility to take him to the Oracle.'

'Yes, my lady,' the councillor bowed and departed gratefully.

'Herakles,' she said addressing the enormous man before her.

'You have me at a disadvantage m' lady,' Herakles replied smiling.

'My name is Athena.' She studied Herakles for any reaction, but there was none. 'I know your father.'

'Then, you must know my mother also?'

'I mean, I know your natural father.'

'I don't understand.'

'Let us sit and take refreshment.' She indicated an establishment that was serving meals and drinks. The place appeared well patronised. 'I will explain it to you, as you now need to learn the truth of your parentage.'

Herakles was hungry and tired. Sitting down to enjoy a meal was a brilliant idea. Sharing it with a beautiful woman seemed an even better one. At the table he ordered a big meal, a jug of wine, and an even larger jug of water. Athena had only the water. Her escorts remained discreetly outside.

'Your father,' she began, 'is not Amphitryon.'

'Yes, he is.' Herakles replied.

'Your actual father is Zeus.'

'Zeus!' Herakles laughed. 'Any particular Zeus, or are you referring to the king of the gods?'

'The Zeus, the main god himself,' she confirmed, smiling back at him, and nodding to the truth of it. She had never had to share this news with anyone before, and the expression of disbelief on Herakles face was entertaining. 'I am his eldest daughter, Athena.'

'If I am his son, and you are his daughter, then that makes us...'

'Brother and sister, of a fashion,' she confirmed.

'So, am I immortal like you?'

'No. You are a demi-god. You are the son of a god and a mortal. You can and will die someday.'

'How did Zeus...?'

'He came to your mother disguised as your father, and he tricked your mother into her bed.' She paused to let that sink in and then added. 'You must understand that it wasn't her fault, she truly believed that she was with Amphitryon.'

Herakles said nothing. He stared blankly at her and continued eating and taking sips of the wine.

'Think of me...' she continued, 'as your much older half-sister.'

Herakles still said nothing.

'Your father, Zeus has spoken to me of that night that he spent with your mother. He does like to boast, even to me.' She smirked at this. 'Please understand...' she paused, 'that you were conceived out of trickery. Hera...'

'Hera?'

'You know of her?'

'She is Zeus's wife. She is the jealous type I believe,' Herakles added.

'She is, and she may well be the cause of your headaches.'

'Oh!' Herakles was a bit confused.

'The Oracle will examine you to confirm it.'

Herakles face portrayed a man who suddenly realised that he knew nothing of his own life.

Athena continued. 'Your parents raised and cared for you as best they could. They did not know that Hera placed a curse on you only days after you were born.'

'I'm cursed, by Hera, for something my father, Zeus, did to my mother,' Herakles was speaking slowly as if bewildered with this surreal explanation.

'Yes. She boasted of doing this to torment Zeus for initiating his indiscretion with your mother.'

'But... I killed my wife and children because of her curse, because of my madness.'

'I'm here, in Delphi, to help you now. I will take you to visit the Oracle, and together we'll the learn the way for you to be rid of your curse.'

'I will be free from headaches?'

'Yes, I believe so. It is the Oracle who will explain how,' she assured him. 'I'll take you to him. But first you should bathe and rest. I'll arrange some clean clothing for you, and you can leave your bag and weapons at my home.'

Herakles considered her many generous offers, and quickly decided that he'd need all of them. He nodded gratefully. 'Can I finish my meal first?' He held up the chunk of bread that he was about to eat and smiled boyishly.

'Of course,' she laughed.

***

The lionesses cave had an acoustic advantage. The cliff opposite the entrance was shaped in such a way that sounds from outside the cave were directed deep into the caves chambers and it acted as an early warning system.

Zosma was grooming herself after a satisfying meal when she heard voices, many voices. She raced out toward the entrance for fear of being trapped inside. She rounded a corner and quickly stopped when she saw that a group of humans had gathered in a circle. She crouched low, flattening her ears, watching them as they heaped wood into a pile in order to make a campfire. This was happening way too close to her den.

She watched a human female stand up and she spoke to one of the men. The lioness watched her walk toward her and so she crouched even lower. As the woman rounded a rock, she removed the lower half of her clothing and squatted. Her urine smell was distinct. By the time the human was finished, the lioness had changed into her human form, and she spoke urgently to the woman. 'Can you please help me?' Zosma whispered.

The female was startled. She did not expect to hear a women's voice. 'Who's there?' she asked looking about her as she hastily re-clothed herself.

Zosma stood up and looked over the rock at the female human. 'I was attacked and raped,' she explained using her distressed voice.

The human female was surprised to see a completely naked woman with long blond hair talking to her, but she said nothing. Immediately the defences were down, and the woman moved slowly toward her and spoke in a calming voice. 'Come with me. I have family and friends here and we will help you.'

'I have a baby,' the lioness lied to her. She looked over her shoulder toward the back of the cave. 'I think my arm is broken and I cannot pick her up or carry her. Can you follow me and bring her out for me?'

'Of course, I will. Where is she?' The woman was now concerned for the infant and wanted to help.

'I have been hiding in this cave... I will show you,' Zosma explained.

'What is your name?' the young woman asked her.

'Zosma,' replied the lioness. 'What is your name?'

'Semele,' she replied. Semele followed Zosma, deeper into the lioness's lair. Even in the relative darkness of the cave the woman saw piles of bones and recognised that many of them were human. Alarmed, she turned to find herself staring into the vivid green eyes of a huge lioness. The lioness swung her mighty paw across her face, and she fell to the ground unconscious. Later, when she awoke, she found herself bound. Confused and dazed she did not see the beast anywhere in the cave. In desperation she called out to the others in the hope of being rescued.

'What's that noise?' the leader of the group accompanying the young woman asked the others.

'I think it was Semele?' answered one of his companions.

The men had been frantically searching for her for some time since she wandered off to do her ablutions. The woman and the five men were on their way into Nemea. Semele was the sister of one of them, and she was going to be married soon. They were escorting her to her future husband and planned to enjoy themselves at the party to celebrate their wedding.

Staying within range of each other they had searched behind rocks, trees and within the cave itself. They feared for her safety as they had heard reports of a giant lioness in these parts. The five men were armed with swords, bows and arrows, and spears. They were all skilled and experienced and had believed they could protect Semele. Now she was missing after simply doing her toilet.

The lioness pounced on the first man. She made no sound and the four others turned to hear muffled sounds of the man being ripped open. As he bled out from his wounds the others attacked. They threw spears but they seemed to just bounce off the lion. Two of the men held up their swords and charged, whilst the other two drew their bows, quivers at the ready. The sword charge failed, as the men stabbed but could not pierce the lion's coat. The lioness roared and standing on her hind legs she swung her razor-sharp claws at both men, slicing their faces and necks open. Both were now dead.

The two bowmen loosened off arrows in quick succession, but the arrows did not penetrate the lion. Looking at each other they fled in different directions. The lion chased down one of the men and leapt from a rock and on to his back. The man died instantly from the crushing impact as his head smashed into the rocky ground. The lioness then leapt up intending to chase down the other fleeing man, but try as she did, she could not see him or pick up his scent.

Puzzled, she returned to examine her fresh kills. She then approached the weeping woman and licked away her salty tears as the woman was now shrieking in extreme panic. The lioness then bit off her head, and the annoying noise abruptly stopped.

***

The Oracle was pleased to grant Herakles an audience.

'I suppose you have been expecting me?' asked Herakles when he was shown into the room where the Oracle sat.

'Why do you suppose that?' the Oracle asked.

'You are an Oracle.' Herakles smiled at his obvious observation.

'I was expecting you, but only because Athena told me you were coming.'

'I thought you could see the future?'

'I can see the past, the present, and the future,' explained the Oracle. 'But first, I must know which direction to look. There is so much to see in the past, that to do so effectively, I must focus on a particular event. The present has so many things happening at any one time, that without specifics, it is just noise. The actions of the many are easy to see, but the actions of a particular individual are very much a challenge, even to me. The future is in permanent flux as it has so many possibilities. I must first learn as much as I can about the situation in order to see its future path with any clarity. Even then, human behaviour can still surprise me,' he explained and smiled.

'But can you see my past, present, and future'?

'I already know a little bit about your past. Athena told me of your real father, and I have heard the stories of your battles, and I know that you have skills with farm animals and working the soil.' The Oracle then paused, and Herakles said nothing. 'Your present is here now with me. Athena already explained that you were staying with her whilst we help you.'

Herakles sat in silence.

'Your future depends on which one of the many paths before you that you choose to take.'

'I had hoped that you would tell me what to do,' Herakles responded.

'Your fate is your own. What do you want to achieve?'

'I want to be rid of these headaches and I want to live a happy life.'

'Tell me about the headaches and what you presently do to abate them?' the Oracle asked and so Herakles explained.

'I drink a mint tea broth. It does seem to help, but I do not enjoy it.'

The Oracle then rose from his chair and crossed the room to where Herakles sat. He placed his hands on Herakles head cupping the scalp with his palms and fingers. After a moment he returned to his seat. 'Herakles, I feel the presence of Hera.'

'Athena told me that she may have cursed me.'

'Do you know her?'

'Not personally. She is my natural father's wife.'

'She is also an exceedingly jealous type of woman. She cannot punish Zeus for his infidelity as he is far too powerful. But she does have a history of punishing his children who were born from the women he takes to bed. I have sensed the presence of a lump that puts pressure on your brain from time to time. It is growing and it will eventually kill you. This is what causes your headaches.'

'What do I do…? How can I be rid of it?'

'I can prescribe you different herbs and medicines to manage the headaches and they'll reduce the severity,'

'My wife….' he paused in the memory of her death. 'The mint tea…'

'A pleasing broth, but as you say, the benefit to you is only temporary,' explained the Oracle. 'Did Chiron prescribe them for you?'

'Yes, he is a tutor that my parents sent me to see to learn from.'

'He is a good man.'

Herakles nodded and stirred restlessly. 'I am ashamed and remorseful for my actions,' he explained.

'Yes. The slaying of your wife and sons must be atoned for,' the Oracle continued. 'You must earn the respect of the people, or you will only be remembered as the bastard son of Zeus who slayed his wife and children.'

'I'll do anything,' Herakles assured him.

'Good,' replied the Oracle. 'The king is a friend of mine and a regular visitor to my chambers.'

Herakles looked at him.

'Eurysthues, King of the Mycenae.' He paused. 'He is your cousin by the way. It is a long story. Anyway, the poor man has a list of problems as long as the Elpeus river. You will agree to help him, and when you do, you will gain the respect, love and admiration of the king and his people. Also, you will gain the respect of your father, Zeus. In time Zeus will take you to Hera and she will rid you from your cursed headaches.'

'I will do this for you and for the king.' Herakles agreed.

'No, no, not for me. Do it for you.' The Oracle told him. 'Now about my fee.'

'I…' Herakles looked embarrassed.

'Do not worry, I already know that you don't have much coin. I do not have to be an Oracle to know that,' he smiled.

Herakles smiled weakly.

'I will offer you to the king as the solution to his problems. We will tell the king that he owes me a reward for finding you. I already know that he will pay me handsomely. Do you agree?'

'Yes, of course.'

'Good.'

The Oracle went to the door and opened it. From the doorway he spoke to someone, and then returned to Herakles. 'I have arranged for a supply of herbs and medicines for you.'

They waited and presently an apothecary arrived at the Oracle's chamber.

'Oracle.'

'Apothecary.'

'I have the herbs and medicines you requested.' He held up a bag. 'Would you like me to examine the patient?' he asked looking at Herakles.

'Thank you, that would be appropriate and appreciated.'

The apothecary walked to Herakles and stopped and stared at him. He looked at the Oracle and asked. 'Zeus?'

'Yes,' the Oracle replied pleasantly surprised.

'And Hera?' he concluded and nodded knowingly.

'Yes,' he confirmed.

The apothecary smiled encouragingly at Herakles. 'Good luck, Herakles. I look forward to learning of your fate.' The apothecary placed the bag in Herakles opened hands, bowed to the Oracle, and left the room.

The Oracle then also walked to the door and by opening it, he motioned that Herakles should also leave, and Herakles concluded that their meeting was now over, stood up to do so.

The Oracle spoke softly to him as he passed. 'I will arrange for you to meet with the king. Athena will go with you. Do not mention that you are cousins, unless he does. You have my best wishes for your future.'

'Thank you,' Herakles bowed and left. He walked through the doorway to the outer rooms of the building, and then departed through the front door to find Athena waiting for him. 'Hello, Athena.'

'Did you learn your fate?'

'I am to assist the king with the problems that persist in his kingdom and thus earn an audience with my father. When I have his respect, he will command Hera to release me from my sufferings.'

'Good plan.' she told him. 'I will arrange for you to meet King Eurysthues. He is a charming man and I'm confident that you'll like and respect him.'

'I only hope he likes me.' Herakles explained his concern.

'Oh, he will love you,' Athena assured him. 'I already know some of the problems he needs fixing and when you do, you will be his hero.'

As Athena and Herakles walked away from Delphi, they discussed the forthcoming meeting.

***

The Hydra named Astron swam the swampy waters in the lagoon at Lerna. As she swam the blood from the fishermen she had just killed, washed off her faces and her body. She liked eating fishermen as she did not have to travel too far to find them. For some reason, they tended to be tastier than other land-dwelling people. Having nine, snakelike heads, made her a fearsome creature, and she was aware that she was held in fear and awe by the local villages that surrounded the lake.

One time, a group of villagers had offered her a naked young woman to her as a sacrifice, seemingly to appease her. She was bound and held steady by two men. The Hydra swam toward them, the young woman pale with fright, and so Astron ate the two men instead. She may be a monster, but it did not mean she didn't have a sense of humour.

***

Herakles and Athena were shown into the king's inner chamber. They were made comfortable seated on large chairs that were covered with lavish cushions. They were served with wine and platters of tasty foods on the table between them. Athena showed a modest restraint choosing to take some of the food out of politeness, but Herakles enthusiastically displayed his hunger, stacked his plate, brimmed his cup, and ate, and drank enough for them both.

The king arrived at the room only when Herakles had had his fill. It seemed that they were being discreetly observed so that Herakles and Athena could feast their fill without reservations or interruption. He entered the room smiling and his arms were up and spread wide in a welcoming gesture. His round beardless face beamed happiness. Herakles and Athena rose to greet the king. In unison, they bowed respectfully toward him.

It was evident that Eurystheus's was excited and extremely pleased to meet with Herakles and Athena. 'Athena! It's so lovely to see you again, as always,' he gushed and affectionately kissed her cheek. Athena inwardly smiled as the king became increasingly familiar every time they met.

'Your majesty. Always a pleasure to be in your company,' she replied with an exaggerated degree of warmth.

Herakles detected Athena's flirtatious voice and discreetly smiled.

'This must be the Herakles who I have heard so much about?' The king asked assessing the man before him. He nodded in appreciation of Herakles muscular bulk and height.

'He is also my brother,' Athena explained as if assuring him of Herakles's credibility.

'You are also welcome in my home,' the king told him.

Herakles said nothing and he sat when the king indicated that he should.

'The Oracle has found you for me, Herakles!' the king exclaimed clapping his hands as if this sealed their relationship. 'How wonderful.'

'Yes,' Herakles agreed.

'I am also told that he arranged medication for you from the apothecary. Is it helping?'

'It is. I haven't felt this well in a long time.'

'Good, good, that's very good.' The king seemed satisfied. 'So, do you willingly undertake to complete these many tasks for me?'

'He will,' answered Athena.

'I must hear Herakles answer for himself.'

'I don't yet know what these tasks are, your majesty,' Herakles replied cautiously.

'They are labours that require your strength, courage, persistence, cunning, and wisdom. Do you have these attributes?' he challenged.

'Yes! He does have these qualities,' chipped in Athena.

'You are an excellent sister, Athena. But please, let the man speak for himself.'

Athena said nothing. She looked towards her younger brother.

Herakles stood and drew to his full height. 'I do have these qualities, but there needs to be one more.'

'Commitment?'

'Yes!'

'If you choose to commit to completing them, and as you succeed in each one, there will be significant rewards for each task completed.'

Herakles smiled, nodded his gratitude, and sat down again.

'For each labour completed, I will reward you commensurate with the amount of danger and difficulty that you encountered. You can also keep what valuables that you salvage, other than the items that your retrieve on my behalf. This will be a bonus and a further reward for yourself. Plus, when you have completed all ten, I'll double the combined total.'

'Ten!'

'Your first labour is to hunt down kill a nuisance lion that has been troubling my shepherds and cattle farmers in Nemea.'

'I have a long bow and sharp arrows that can easily kill a lion.'

'Excellent. Then you should not have too much trouble.'

'Offer him land,' Athena said to the king.

The king looked Athena and then slowly turned to look at Herakles.

Herakles nodded slightly.

'Very well,' the king sighed. 'When you complete your list, I will also grant you a sizable plot of quality farming land.'

Athena asked, 'How large?'

'I do not know yet!' the king was now becoming exasperated. 'I will have to consider which parcel of land to give him,' replied the king. 'Complete these labours to my satisfaction, and the land will be yours. I can afford to be generous.'

'Make certain it will be big enough and fertile enough for me to grow crops and farm sheep and cattle,' Herakles added.

'It will be, I promise,' responded the king. 'And the soil will be productive, and it will be along a river, and it will be close to the markets, and you will have the necessary labourers to make it work.'

'And you will put all of these commitments in writing,' Athena added.

'And I will put pen to paper committing myself to these terms,' he agreed, looking harangued.

'Now, you have my full commitment,' Herakles said proudly as he stood up. "I am ready to start,' he said smiling, very pleased with the proffered terms.

'Good.' The king paused considering. 'Do you need staff? Litter bearers, porters, guards, supplies, that sort of thing?'

'No sir. I travel alone.'

'I will watch over him,' Athena assured smiling.

'Very good,' he said also smiling but also looking relieved. A retinue of staff for Herakles would have cost him a fortune. Though, he could have deducted this expense from his reward. 'When will you leave?'

'Today, point me towards the location of the Nemean lion.'

They all laughed.

Herakles rose and he and the king firmly held each other's arms sealing their agreement. They separated and Herakles headed for the door. The king then spoke. 'Herakles.'

Herakles stopped and turned. 'Yes, my king?'

'They will sing your praises.'

'How do you mean?'

'The people, as you complete these labours, they'll sing your praises. People will compose songs and tell stories about you. They will honour you for decades to come. You will become the hero to the people of these lands.'

'The ten labours of Herakles,' Athena said as she nodded agreeing. 'A worthy quest.'

'Some coin, a farm, and a house to call home is all that I want.' And with a nod and a wink, Herakles departed.

Athena bade her farewell to the king and then quickly followed Herakles.

***

Their journey to Nemea was uneventful. Athena went with him as far as the village. As they walked, she told him about key events in his extended family's history. Mostly Herakles listened in silence. Learning that his natural father was the prominent God, was a difficult concept to come to terms with. He had heard the stories of Mount Olympus and the Gods, everyone had, but to discover that he himself was a demi-god was a lot to absorb. He wondered how he would feel when they eventually met.

When they arrived in Nemea, Athena set about securing suitable lodgings for them. The villagers were curious about them and soon a crowd had surrounded the two of them as they dined at the one public eatery that served food.

'Who are you?' one asked above the chatter.

'I am Herakles, and this is, Athena,' Herakles answered for them.

They laughed and Herakles and Athena gave each other a bewildered look.

'Why are you here?' another asked.

'To make babies!' added one other, and they all erupted in laughter.

Herakles found a crate to stand on. He stood above the crowd and looked impressive with his muscular body and his weaponry. 'I am here to kill a lion that has been attacking your sheep and cattle. Do you know of it?'

The villagers went quiet. 'It was nice meeting you,' one man finally spoke out.

'That lioness has killed many of our villager's also,' another added.

'It killed my family,' another added. 'And it very nearly killed me.'

'You have seen it?'

'Yes,' he continued. 'This lioness is bigger, stronger, faster, and more cunning than all others. We have hunted lions before, but none such as this.'

'Where will I find it?' Herakles asked.

As a group they all pointed west.

'Then that's the direction I'll go. Tomorrow morning I'll go and kill the lioness!'

One person started to cheer, but he quickly realised that he was alone in his praise and abruptly ceased.

***

Herakles knew he was getting close when he saw the mutilated remains of livestock. He found a place where a cow had been killed and determined by the freshness of the kill that it had happened only that morning. Now birds pecked greedily at its remnants, flies swarmed, and ants were stripping the meat from the carcass.

He checked the wind. It was to his back, and he hoped his scent wouldn't give him away. Herakles saw the lionesses paw prints leading away from the area and set about following the spoor. Herakles was exceptionally quiet when he hunted. He maintained his stealthy trek deep into the woods for many hours without sighting the monstrous lioness. The whole time, his bow was in his hand, and he had his reinforced arrows ready to nock and release.

'Who are you?' a woman's voice asked him.

Herakles was startled. He was tensed up looking for a vicious lioness to kill, and instead, he heard a sweet female voice. 'Herakles,' he answered to the breeze. 'Where are you?'

'Here,' she replied, and the woman's head appeared above a rock. She was smiling as she clambered awkwardly up to the top of the rock.

She was magnificent thought Herakles. Her emerald-green eyes were captivating. She had long golden hair which caught the sunlight and glowed. She was tall, slender, and gorgeous. She was wearing a short dress made from skins that barely covered her breasts and buttocks, and Herakles found himself mesmerised by the sight of her.

'Why are you here, Herakles?'

'I had thought to kill a lion, but it could be that I'm here to rescue you, and perhaps win your affections.'

'Do I look like I need rescuing?' she asked coyly.

Herakles looked about the area. 'No,' he conceded, but then added, 'I suppose you don't. Pity.'

The young woman leapt from the rock and landed sure footed in front of Herakles. 'But you do want my affections?' she asked him sweetly.

Herakles considered the question. It had been some time since he had been with a woman, and she was desirable. But then he hesitated. He thought that perhaps he did not want to be distracted by offers of sex when he should be focused on hunting a lioness.

'I think I do, I really do, but first I need to kill the lioness,' he explained.

'The lioness left this region a long time ago,' the woman informed him.

'I saw its recent kill,' Herakles replied, and he was confused by what she claimed.

'Wild dogs,' she explained.

Herakles said nothing. He had never heard of wild dogs ripping flesh in the manner that he had just seen.

'I have reports that its hunting grounds are just west from here.'

'Then you should continue west,' she answered and turned to gaze in that direction.

Herakles said nothing. He stared at her, and she smiled.

Perhaps the lioness has returned to these parts.

'I should continue...'

'It will be dark soon...' she countered. 'You could rest with me tonight, and continue your hunt at dawn, feeling refreshed and per-haps... satisfied.'

Her suggestion had merit and she was beautiful. 'Do you have a camp? Or are you out here alone?' Herakles asked.

'Herakles, you do ask a lot of questions.'

'What is your name?'

'Zosma,' she answered. 'Enjoy me right now, or forever lose the opportunity,' she invited him teasingly.

Herakles still hesitated. 'I have no coin to pay you,' he explained to her.

'I do not want your coins! I want to have babies!'

'From me?'

'Why not? You look healthy, strong, and brave. I believe these are good qualities in a seed father.'

'I cannot stay out here to live with you,' he explained.

'I do not want a husband,' she added laughing just some cu...,' She hesitated 'err, bubs to call my own.'

Herakles dropped his weapons and started to remove his clothing.

Zosma whooped in delight. She threw off the dress and went down on her hands and knees proffering her sex toward him. He was quickly aroused and penetrated her with ease. His thrusts became urgent, and he did not last long. Almost at once, his seed was spent.

He withdrew feeling a little lightheaded, and he was a bit disappointed that it was all over so quickly.

'There,' she purred. 'Wasn't that pleasant?'

'Oh Yes! I thank you dear lady,' he said smiling, 'but I cannot promise you that we have made a baby.'

'The gods will soon tell us,' She assured him, but she was smiling happily as if knowing it to be already true.

Herakles said nothing.

'Why do you want to kill the lioness?' she asked him as she stood facing him, legs slightly apart. She could tell that her posture held Herakles complete attention and she smiled at the effect her body held over him.

Herakles realised he had been staring and almost shook himself into answering. 'For me, it's about the rewards,' he answered, and then he added. 'For the people of Nemea, it is about stopping the killing of their families and friends, and their sheep and cattle.'

'But I am sure that the lioness only kills to defend and feed herself,' she justified.

'If and when the lioness finds a mate, she will produce a litter, then soon there will be many lions killing in these parts. It is better to stop them before they multiply, and whilst there is only one.'

'How will you kill the lioness?'

'I have my bow and arrow,' he answered. 'And I also have my spear and a sword if it comes to that.'

'I wish you well,' said Zosma.

'Thank you, Zosma. I wish you well also,' he said as he looked intently at her naked body some more. Every feature of her was tantalising and he knew it would not take him long to become aroused again. She seemed comfortable talking with him and he realised that he too was still undressed, and that it did not concern him. He then noticed that she was smiling at him, clearly pleased the effect that her nakedness was having on him.

She spoke gently, as if wanting to maintain the mood. 'I will fetch some food and a blanket from my camp and bring it here to lay with you. Could you gather some firewood? It will be a cold night.'

'I will,' he assured her, and he was now rising to his feet also.

They gathered their clothing. Zosma only took a moment to slip on her dress and she headed off with a smile and a wave of her hand.

Herakles dressed and collected his weapons. He then gathered the firewood that was close at hand, but he soon realised that he would have to search farther out to have a sufficient pile to last the night. He walked close to the rock where he first saw Zosma and found several long branches that were very suitable for burning. He gathered them into a heap and scooped them in his arms when he heard a roar of a lion just as it jumped upon him from the rocks. He ducked. The fire-wood was rough and jagged, and it deflected the lioness's pounce. The lioness landed and turned, growling at Herakles who had gathered his spear and thrust it strongly toward the lions hide, but it did not pene-trate.

The lioness withdrew two paces and crouched down ready to pounce again. Herakles held his spear up with its base in the ground ready to take the weight of the attacking lioness on the point of the spear, but the lioness checked herself and turned left, jumping, and then swinging back. Herakles now had his sword and used the sun-light's reflection off the shiny steel to dazzle the lioness, and in her confusion, she turned and ran away. Herakles quickly nocked his ar-rows and drew his bow. He had time to let three arrows fly before she was out of range. All three found their target, but none had pene-trated the lionesses hide.

Herakles then climbed the rocks so that he could watch the direc-tion that the lioness took and was surprised to find Zosma's dress ly-ing on the ground. There was no blood and no tearing. Herakles was confused at first. He then concluded by the madness of the gods, that the lioness and Zosma were one and the same. Then the realisation of what he had done with her occurred to him, as the blood drained from his face, he hoped he had not just fathered lion cubs.

Herakles was astounded that his spear and his arrows had not hurt the lion. Herakles then decided he needed a new weapon. He looked about him. The firewood had deflected the lion. Maybe a wooden club would work. If he could swing the club onto the lioness's head with enough force, he may be able to kill it, or at least knock it uncon-scious.

Herakles quickly found the timber that approximated the shape of a club. In the darkness and cold he worked furiously reshaping the club using his knife and sword to whittle it into shape. He would need to resharpen both blades before using them in a battle. He examined the club. It had to fit both of his hands on the handle, and it had to be long enough to avoid the reach of the lion's claws and teeth. It also had to be heavy enough so that in its momentum it would do damage, but it could not be too heavy so that he couldn't comfortably lift it to use it. Soon the club was finished, and Herakles positioned it into the tree with the handle pointing outward for easy accessibility.

Herakles then urinated in several locations. Next, he rubbed leaves and mud onto his skin masking his scent. He walked back to the club bearing tree and with his back to the tree he sat down and relaxed enough to fall into a light sleep. As the dawn light touched his face, he heard a noise. Without moving his arms or legs he slowly opened his eyes. The lioness was close, looking for him. He knew his scent was everywhere and the air was still, and this would help to confuse her. Both were hungry and both were determined to win the battle. Their own lives depended on it.

'Zosma!' Herakles called.

The lioness now looked in his direction. She was about thirty paces away.

The time that it took Herakles to stand up, was the same amount of time that it took for the lioness to reach him at full charge. Herakles reached up, grabbed the handle of the club, and swung it down hard onto the lioness's head, all whilst doing his best to avoid its outstretched claws. The impact was devastating for the beast and the lioness collapsed into a dead heap. It had only taken Herakles one blow of his club to kill the monster. Perhaps they would sing songs about him after all.

It was then that he noticed his bloody hand. One of her claws had scratched his finger. It began to hurt painfully now that he knew he was wounded. He bound his hand expertly. He had been wounded many times before and he knew what to do.

Herakles knew he needed evidence that the animal was defeated. He decided that a strip of the lionesses' pelt would be convincing, so he drew his knife and started to cut, but it would not pierce the pelt. He got his sword and stabbed at her, but again it did not cut through the lioness's hide. Herakles was confused, but them he remembered that he had blunted both blades when he fashioned the club. Patiently he worked the knife with the sharpening stone until he was satisfied that it was ready. He then tried again on the pelt, but despite using all his strength, the pelt would not cut.

He sat for a moment in stunned silence. Perhaps if he fetched Athena, she could be his witness to the monster's fate. Checking once more that the lioness had no pulse, he was surprised to find one, the beast was not dead.

Gripping her neck in both hands Herakles squeezed. He held the neck tightly for several minutes and then he checked for a pulse once more. No, there was none. Herakles then gathered his bag and his weapons, and hurriedly left the scene of the battle to fetch Athena.

He travelled quickly and without incident. His arrival at the village was greeted with both surprise and happiness. Athena was also there to greet him. He got onto the crate that he had stood on only two days before, and he addressed the crowd.

'I have today fought the lioness and I have defeated it. The lioness is dead.'

The crowd roared in delight. They cheered and shouted 'Herakles, Herakles,' repeatedly.

He stepped off the crate and Athena held out her hand. He showed her the cut finger and she took him to her room to attend to the wound with ointments she had brought with her.

'Will this affect your use of your weapons?' she was concerned.

'No, I don't think so. I fight equally well with both hands.' Herakles assured her.

Athena said nothing. A great warrior always practiced weapon use with both hands. They used both hands, elbows, knees, feet, and even their head, as required to defeat their enemy.

'So, the first task is completed?' she asked him as she wound the bandage over the injury protecting it from infection. She completed the task and looked at Herakles.

'Yes,' he replied grinning. He held up the bandaged hand. 'Thank you,' he acknowledged her ministrations.

'You will need proof of the kill,' she recommended him.

'I wanted to bring the king a strip of the pelt, but I could not cut through the hide of the lion,' he informed her. 'I thought if you could be my witness to its dead remains, then that should be sufficient? He trusts you.'

Athena nodded. 'Take me to the lioness and show me where it lays, and I will be your witness,' Athena agreed.

Herakles and Athena set out. They both understood the urgency and wanted to prove his claim before anyone moved the carcass. They soon arrived at the scene of the fight, but the lioness's body was gone.

'Stolen!' Herakles said collapsing to the ground in resignation.

Athena looked at the site where Herakles had struck the beast.

'I don't see any "thieves" footprints,' she told him.

Herakles stood up and scanned the area.

'There are only lion prints,' he concluded. He pointed, 'They lead off that way.'

'Herakles...' Athena admonished him. 'You may have fought the lion, but you did not kill it. It faked its own demise and then fled when you left.'

'But...' Herakles was exasperated. 'There was no heartbeat.'

'You should track the beast while the trail is fresh.'

'Yes, of course. Will you return to the village?'

'No, I think I'll go with you so that I can witness the kill.'

'I will protect you.'

'I know that to be true,' she laughed. 'But I can protect myself,' she slapped the hilt of her own sword.

Herakles picked up the huge wooden club, rested it over his shoulder, and he set off following the trail left by the lioness with Athena following close behind him. She fell back a few paces after Herakles had come close to accidently hitting her with the club as he turned left or right whilst focusing on tracking the lioness. He came to a place where there were fallen weapons scattered on the rocks. A detailed examination found blood also. Herakles looked about and spotted the entrance to the cave. He went nearer to it and was almost overwhelmed by the smell of death and decay that wafted out of it.

Herakles went back to Athena. 'Could you scale those rocks?' He pointed to a high rocky outcrop.

She looked up and nodded. 'Yes,' she added.

'From the top I want you to call out, "Zosma, help me!" as loud as you can.'

Athena turned and climbed the rocks. Stealthily, Herakles went to stand at the side of the cave entrance where he waited with his club poised high above his head. Athena waved to indicate that she was ready, and Herakles nodded.

'Zosma, help me!' Athena shouted.

Nothing happened.

'Zosma, please help me. I'm trapped, and my leg, it really hurts,' Athena continued making her voice seem distressed and especially vulnerable.

Zosma soon appeared at the caves entrance. She was naked and Herakles was surprised to see her come outside in her human form. He involuntarily gasped when he saw the bulge in her belly. Zosma turned toward the sound and saw Herakles brandishing the club. She kicked wildly at Herakles groin, but Herakles had quickly turned, and her foot landed on his thigh. As she pivoted away from him, she instantly changed into her lioness form as the swing of his club dealt the lioness a savage blow on her hip. Her hip bone was now severely smashed, and the injured lioness turned with some difficulty and obvious pain. She turned to try to bite Herakles, but she was now too slow. Herakles did an upper cut thrust with the club, striking the jawbone and sending the lioness sprawling. He next raised the club high and brought it down hard. This final blow to her head made a cracking sound as he split the fur covered skull. Fountains of blood now spurted in all directions from her wounds.

The lioness now lay motionless, defeated, dying. He knelt beside it and wrapped his giant hands around its neck and squeezed, holding the air pipe closed until he was satisfied that the monster was truly dead.

Athena had climbed down from her high point. She came up to Herakles and embraced him. 'Well fought brother.'

'Now, I do believe that I have truly defeated this lioness,' he exclaimed still panting.

'As your witness, I can confirm that you did,' she said smiling. 'Why don't you skin it, as proof?'

'My knife will not be able to cut the pelt,' Herakles explained.

She touched the fur of the lioness and nodded. 'Why don't you use the lionesses' own claws to cut through the fur?' she suggested.

Herakles squatted beside the giant paw of the lioness. He picked up the claw and extended it. Using his knife, he managed to cut off the toe, and he then pushed the extended claw into the flesh. 'Hmm...' he murmured. 'That seems to be working.'

Starting at the neck and using the lionesses' own claws, Herakles removed the pelt from the lioness. It took many hours. Athena had found a stream and they took the pelt to it and washed away the blood and fat that remained. Herakles prepared a fire and they cooked, and ate, the flesh of the rabbits he had caught. They discussed eating the lioness, but it did not seem right.

By mid-morning, the pelt was almost dry. Herakles next fashioned the skin as a coat. He had decided that if the king did not want the coat, he would keep it for himself. It would be good armour and would give him some protection from the blades and arrows of those he fought in battle. It would also keep him warm and dry. Herakles and Athena then set off to the village. They were eager to share the news that the lioness was now defeated, and that the villagers and their livestock were now safe.

As they came near to the cave where the dead lioness lay, Athena spoke Herakles. 'Go on ahead without me,' she told him.

He looked at her.

'I want to say a few words of remembrance at this momentous place,' she explained.

'I should stay with you,' he offered.

'I will be quite safe,' she told him.

Herakles could tell that she wanted to be alone with the body of the lioness. He nodded his understanding.

'I shouldn't be long,' she motioned for him to go.

Herakles shrugged and walked off.

Athena waited for a few moments and then called. 'Zeus!'

Nothing happened.

'Zeus!' she called even louder.

'What?' A voice boomed from everywhere.

'It is me, Athena,' she told him.

'I know it is you,' he replied.

'Come here,' she commanded.

Zeus appeared. 'What do you want? I was busy,' he said complaining.

'I can imagine,' said Athena. 'Look at this,' she said pointing to the skinned bloodied remains of the lioness that Herakles had killed.

'What about it?'

'Your son, Herakles defeated her in a mighty battle. He was clever, resourceful, and impressively brave.'

'Was that the lioness child of Typhon and Echidna?' asked Zeus.

'Yes,' she replied.

'They are creative,' said Zeus. 'I have their eagle child doing some work for me on Prometheus's liver.'

'I know.'

'The fur is missing,' he observed pointing at the lioness's carcass.

'Herakles is wearing it,' replied Athena.

'I have never eaten lion,' declared Zeus. 'Does it taste any good?' he inquired.

'I think it is an acquired taste,' she told him. 'But we did not try it, so I do not know.'

Zeus nodded. 'Thanks for showing me... I guess.' he trailed off.

'I want you to commemorate it into the heavens.' she told him.

'Why don't you do it?' he asked dryly.

'You are his father,' she explained. 'It would mean more if you did it.'

'If this beast...,' said Zeus indicating the lion once more, '...did so much killing and terrorising,' he continued, 'why should we commemorate it?

'It's symbolic of Herakles great victory over the animal.'

'Herakles is a big, strong, and exceptionally cunning warrior. What makes you say it is a great victory?'

'Neither arrow, nor blade, could penetrate this lioness hide. Herakles had to be smart to find the solution. So, he fashioned a wooden club and pounded the lioness. He then strangled it with his bare hands until it was dead.'

'Was he wounded during the battle?'

'His hand was bleeding. I tended to it. Why?'

'Spilled blood peppers a legend.'

'There was blood.'

'Very well.'

Zeus drew himself to his full height and thrust is hand high toward the skies.

'I Zeus, king of all the gods, cast the image of this lion into the heavens to commemorate the glory of my son, Herakles's victory over it, thereby....' He was looking at Athena for inspiration.

'...Thereby protecting the people and their livestock.' Athena coached him along.

'...Thereby protecting the people and their livestock.' Zeus repeated.

'...Of the people of Nemea.' Athena continued.

'...Of the people of Nemea!' Zeus repeated, his voice now booming loudly in conclusion.

'Is that it?' she asked him.

'Tonight, when you look to the stars you will all see it. It will glow quite bright for a number of years and the story of how Herakles defeated the lioness will become a famous legend across all the lands,'

Zeus explained. 'I might help the story along with a few utterances of it, as I am certain that you will also.'

Athena smiled at him. 'I am impressed father. Thank you.'

'Also,' Zeus continued, 'I will have a gift for Herakles.'

'What is it?'

'A sword. One strong enough and sharp enough to deal with problems like this,' he indicated the lionesses corpse. 'You will find it on the path when you next journey out.'

'I will present it to your son in your name,' Athena assured him.

'Are you coming to Mount Olympus soon?'

'No. Herakles still needs me, and I want to help him,' she told him, and then added. 'Can you rid him of his headaches?'

'No, only Hera can do that,' he replied. 'And sadly, for Herakles, killing a nasty lioness and doing other good deeds will not impress her very much.'

'Why did you marry her?'

'Seemed like a good idea at the time,' he answered with a muted reply.

Athena looked at him dourly.

'I was aroused, and well, she wanted commitment,' he explained, winked, and then he quickly departed.

Athena looked one last time at the lioness's body. She thought it undignified that it should be just left there to decay. But she accepted that it was too big for her to move. Ants and flies now swarmed all over it, and its decay would soon attract other carrion. She bowed her head in salute, and then turned to follow Herakles to the village.

***

Zeus returned home to Mount Olympus where he was at once confronted by his wife, Hera.

'Where have you been?' she demanded.

'Athena asked me to visit her,' Zeus replied. Athena was a daughter he had fathered from another woman, long before he married Hera. She was the type of woman that everyone respected and even Hera liked her.

'What did she want?' Hera relaxed, now knowing that Zeus had not been in bed with yet another woman. She hated his infidelity.

'She is assisting Herakles in completing challenging tasks. He just defeated the lioness at Nemea and Athena wanted me to see the dead monster and acknowledge Herakles victory over it.'

'Herakles, I placed a curse on him. How does he still survive?'

'Why you punish my children for my indiscretions, I will never understand,' Zeus looked tired.

'Their suffering is a warning to all other woman not to bed my husband,' Hera explained.

'How is that working out for you?' Zeus admonished.

Hera said nothing. She looked at Zeus and decided she would intercede when Herakles was next in peril. She would end his life, but not by her own hand, as Zeus would get angry with her if he believed that she had personally killed him. Zeus was protective of the children that he liked, and it seemed that he both liked and respected Herakles.

***

The Hydra, Astron, swam in lazy circles near the surface of the clear water. She was feeling both bored and peckish. The local people no longer swam in her lake and the fisherman had left. Or had she eaten them? She did not know or understand. The larger fish were already eaten, and the smaller fish were too difficult to catch. Even the ducks had stopped visiting. She would have to eat soon and thought on that problem as she glided through the water. She could turn into human form and look for humans or animals to kill and eat, but she had no real strength when she was in her human form. Then an idea slowly came to her. Perhaps as a human, she could get them to follow her into the water.

When Astron reached the decision to leave the safety of the lake to entice prey, it seemed an urgent thing do. The solution she devised apparently increased her appetite. She swam to the shore and morphed into a human woman. She stepped out of the lake and onto dry land. It felt strangely exhilarating. She had not been in human form since first arriving at the lake and that was too long ago for her to remember it clearly. The sun wrapped about her naked body, and she felt herself drying and getting warmer. Heat weakened her, so she resolved not to venture too far from the water. Next, she set off walking toward where she knew the human village was situated. Astron hoped she could find a cow or perhaps a sheep and then lead it into the water to eat it. Presently, a young man came walking toward her.

Her first instinct was to hide, but she fought her initial concern and kept walking confidently toward him.

He stopped and stared at her. She was very tall with slim features. He calculated from her perky breasts that she was about twenty years old. She looked innocent and in need of protection. Her jet-black hair was long and shiny, and her skin tone was pale, despite walking about disrobed. He thought she had easily become sunburned. 'You should not walk about naked,' he told her sounding concerned. He looked about to see if there was anyone else present that could see her. They were alone.

'Oh, sorry,' she replied, as if forgetting that she was.

'It will give men the wrong impression about you,' he added, trying hard not to look at her smallish breasts or the wispy curls of her pubic area.

'About what?' she asked.

'That you have been forcibly disrobed and molested.'

She shook her head.

'Or, that you want to fornicate.'

They were now closing in on each other and stopped within a couple of paces of each other. 'What is fornicate?' she asked him.

'Oh,' he said. 'You are a virgin?'

'Is that a good thing to be?' she asked as she stepped closer to him. He looked uncomfortable.

'I guess,' he considered. 'But if you want to remain one, you really should put some clothes on.' He reached into a bag, found a shirt, and offered it to her.

She shook her head and declined. 'I have clothes of course,' she explained. 'But I took them off when I went swimming.'

'That lake is a dangerous place to swim,' he told her whilst looking at the water. 'There is a monstrous nine headed sea snake that lives in there.'

'I was swimming for quite some time... but I didn't see anything scary,' She explained.

'Maybe the monster is asleep.'

'It's so very hot!' she declared.

'You really should put this on,' he said holding the shirt out toward her.

'Do you want to molest me?'

'No!'

'Why not? Am I not attractive enough?'

'You are attractive,' he explained, nodding his appreciation of her. 'But I don't molest women.'

'Don't you like girls?' she teased.

'Of course, I do,' he answered offended. 'It is just that I like to get to know them for a while before I lay down with them.'

'Would you like to go for a swim with me?' she invited him.

He hesitated.

'The monster is not in the water, I promise you.' She smiled intending to disarm him.

His tense body visibly relaxed. 'Very well,' he agreed, but the uncertainty was still evident in his voice. 'It is getting warm, and I have not been swimming for a long time,' he paused and then grinned. 'And I really could do with a wash.'

The urge of getting to know this beautiful and delightfully naked young woman appealed strongly to him. Perhaps a swim would be a good way to get to know her. He followed her to the water's edge and stopped. She was already ankle deep in the water and she had seen him hesitate. 'Are you worried about the monster?'

'Yes, and so should you.'

'You should get undressed before you get into the water.'

'Oh.'

'You will want dry clothes to put on when we are finished.'

'Yes, I suppose you are right.' He turned to look for somewhere to disrobe.

'What are you looking for?'

'Somewhere where I can take my clothes off.'

'I am naked. Doesn't that mean I get to see you naked too?' she teased.

Hesitantly he dropped his packs and then quickly got undressed.

'Maybe you should hide your clothes,' she recommended him.

'Why?'

'In case someone decides to steal them,' she laughed and then added, 'You will not fit into any of mine.'

He felt her gaze on his body and became self-conscious. She laughed again as he tried to hide his genitals from her. 'Do not worry so much. I won't see them when you are in the water,' she told him.

'They don't shrink that much,' he defended.

He then found a crook in a tree and placed his clothes into his bag and into the tree. He turned and ran into the water. He dived under, turned, and surfaced to see her diving in behind him. Her bum sank beneath the water and then her head appeared out of the water beside him.

'I don't even know your name.'

'Call me Astron,' she replied.

'I am called 'Hem,' he informed her.

'Very nice to meet you Hem,' she laughed.

He dived under the water and swam away from her. He surfaced and looked toward her uncertain of what to say or do next.

'I'll race you to that log,' she pointed to a floating log farther out into the lake.

'That's a long way out,' he replied.

'Too far for you?' she teased.

He turned and swam for the log. She was behind him, and he wanted to impress her so he exerted greater effort. He was first to reach the log, and he turned to see her some distance off. She waved and then sunk beneath the water. He waited and waited and then he got concerned for her. Sudden movement from below the water attracted his attention and he became worried that the monster had taken her. He suddenly felt he was a long way from the shore, when a snake head reached out of the water and grabbed his head in its jaws, silencing him mid-scream. A second head grabbed an arm and a third a leg. The Hydra lifted Hem from the water and shook him as it tore his body apart. A fourth and fifth head joined in the attack shedding the limbs from the torso. Astron in her Hydra form sank beneath the surface and swam happily. Her plan had worked, and she had eaten. She would use this method again.

***

Herakles and Athena reached the city gates and received a joyous welcome from the people. The news of his victory over the lioness had preceded them. People now lined the streets, and they were cheering and waving and calling out Herakles name. One young man shouted above the crowd and jumped out before them. 'Uncle!' he cried.

'Iolaus!' Herakles exclaimed in happy surprise, and they embraced.

'What are you doing here?' Herakles asked him.

'Looking for you, of course.'

'That's fantastic!' He turned to Athena. 'This is my nephew, Iolaus.' he told her.

'It is a pleasure to meet you, Iolaus. My name is Athena,' she told him.

'Is she…?' Iolaus was curious.

'Herakles knew that look. 'She is my sister,' he explained.

'Oh.' He did not know he had an auntie. He decided not to ask about her in her presence. He smiled at his uncle. 'I want to hear everything about your adventures!' Iolaus demanded enthusiastically.

The three of them journeyed farther into the city with Iolaus asking many questions about his battle with the fierce lioness. Herakles laughed in reply. He was so happy to see his nephew and was happily sharing his story when they came across a palace official who stood waiting for them in the market square. 'Welcome Herakles, welcome Athena' he said and bowed respectfully.

'Thank you,' Athena spoke for them.

'News of your victory over the lioness has proceeded you. His majesty waits to honour you and reward your feat.'

'My feet?' Herakles looked down, puzzled.

'Feat! Your victory over the lioness!' Iolaus explained.

'Oh,' he winked and smiled.

Iolaus howled with laughter at his uncle's joke. Athena shook her head and smiled.

'Is this man with you?' asked the official.

'This is my nephew, Iolaus,' Herakles told him. 'He comes with us.'

The official nodded his consent and turned toward the palace. They followed him through the gates into the palace grounds. The crowds cheered and waved but did not follow them in. Once the gates were secured by the palace guards, the king emerged from the main doorway. 'Herakles, my champion!' he declared.

They held arms and then the king turned and embraced Athena. 'Who is this?' the king asked looking at Iolaus.

Herakles did the introductions and Iolaus did an exaggerated bow.

'After you have eaten and rested, I will show you my appreciation,' Eurystheus announced.

Herakles and Athena were shown into a suite with many rooms and beds. Bathing vessels had been filled with hot water, and food was piled up on a table that was surrounded with comfortable chairs. Both Herakles and Athena indulged in a bath, then food, wine and eventually sleep. Iolaus happily attended to both of them.

The following day the king informed them that Herakles had earned much gold coin and it would be kept in safe keeping. 'You must proceed with great haste to your next task, Herakles's King Eurystheus told them.

'What is it great King?' Herakles asked him.

'There is a water snake terrorising the people of Lerna.

'A snake?'

'A Hydra,' explained Athena. 'It is another monster child of Typhon and Echidna.'

'Apparently it is enormous.' added Eurystheus.

'Its breath is fiery and has toxic fumes,' continued, Athena.

'And it has nine heads,' the king added.

'All with razor sharp teeth,'

Whilst Herakles looked doubtful, Iolaus whooped in excited anticipation.

'You'll have no trouble at all,' said the king, encouragingly.

***

The following morning, they all gathered for breakfast.

'I really don't want you to come with me on this quest,' Herakles explained to Iolaus.

'Yes, you do,' he replied.

'Er, no I don't,' countered Herakles.

'You do… you just don't realise it yet,' Iolaus smiled.

'It's too dangerous.'

'Danger shared is danger halved,' Iolaus countered

'Athena! Please explain it to him,' Herakles was getting exasperated.

'I think it's highly appropriate that Iolaus should be with us. This is a dangerous mission, and three swords are better than one,' Athena replied.

'Are you certain you don't want help carrying that?' Herakles showed the long narrow box that Athena had carried since they left Tiryn.

'No thank you. I will manage, just fine,' she answered with a forced grin.

'Why won't you tell us what it is?' Herakles pleaded.

'I've already explained to you that I will tell you when the time is right.'

'And now is not the right time,' added Iolaus laughing.

'You're no help.'

'But I am here to help. That is the whole point,' he retorted, feigning hurt.

Presently they came across a family group walking toward them. They walked in silence as the two groups drew closer together. They were about to pass each other when the man turned to them and asked. 'I beg you, please tell me…' he asked hesitatingly. 'Are you Herakles?'

They stopped and Herakles replied. 'I am.'

'And are you here to kill the Hydra?'

'Yes, we are.' added Iolaus.

'What do you know of that?' Herakles asked.

'News of your task has preceded you Herakles. We welcome you and bid you a safe accomplishment of it.'

'Where are you heading?' Athena asked curiously.

'Naupliē.' The man answered. 'My wife has family there, and it is no longer safe to live near the lake.'

'Why do people live near the lake when there is so much danger from the monster?' Herakles wanted to know.

'The lake is fed by a freshwater spring. It is near the sea, so people live there to fish and raise their families, but they need the fresh water from the lake to drink. We are leaving, the monster has driven us away from our home.'

'Thank you for explaining this to me. I will make the water safe for everyone. Is it much farther to the lake?'

'It is not far. You will soon be there. I bid you all well.' The man studied them, nodded, and then motioned for his family to hurry away.

'Not far to go now, Athena.'

'I heard. I think we should rest before you fight the Hydra,' she suggested.

'I say we press on. The sooner we defeat it, the sooner we can celebrate,' countered Iolaus.

'I'm too agitated to rest,' added Herakles. 'I agree, let us press on.'

As they continued walking toward the lake Herakles asked Athena a question. 'I only know a little about you Athena. Who was your mother?' he asked.

'My mother's name is Metis...' she began.

'A Titan?' exclaimed Herakles.

'Yes,' she answered. 'She was a Titaness of good council, advice, planning and wisdom.'

'Then you have much to thank her for,' concluded Herakles.

Iolaus countered. 'I thought you were born as an adult from Zeus's head. I heard you already had all your armour and weapons and challenged the first man you saw to a fight!'

Athena laughed. 'That is only a fanciful story, Iolaus. I'm sure even Zeus himself enjoys hearing it, but it is not true.'

Iolaus looked disappointed and Herakles laughed at the crestfallen look on his face. They walked in silence for some time then Iolaus exclaimed to Athena questioningly, 'But you fought in the Titanomarchy!'

'I did,' she agreed and was about to explain, but they had arrived at the lake. They dropped their bags in a pile and began looking out for the monster.

'This lake is much bigger than I had imagined,' Herakles murmured.

'It is estimated to be five thousand paces from side to side. They say it has no bottom and that the depths descends to Hades itself,' Athena explained.

'How do we find the beast?' asked Iolaus.

'Perhaps we could call out for it,' Herakles replied mockingly. 'Woo-hoo, monster! Come and get us. Would you care to join us in a battle to the death?'

'That might actually work,' laughed Athena.

A young woman approached them. She was wearing men's clothing. 'Can I help you?' she asked showing concern. 'You look lost,' she continued.

'We have been told there is a nine headed Hydra swimming in this lake,' Herakles replied. 'We'd like to make its acquaintance.'

'There is!' she exclaimed. 'It is a massively nasty one. It eats people you know?'

'We have heard,' Iolaus explained to her smiling, clearly attracted to her. 'Do you know how we can find it?'

'I suppose… you could just call out for it,' she suggested smiling whilst gazing suggestively back at Iolaus.

'See!' Herakles said to Iolaus but he said nothing. They looked at Athena and she was clearly tired and needed to rest.

'What is your name?' asked Iolaus.

'I'm called, Astron,' she informed him.

'Do you live in these parts?'

'I live here, by the lake.'

'Doesn't the monster frighten you?'

'In all my years of living here, I've never actually seen the monster,' she laughed.

'Maybe the monster has already died of old age,' Iolaus suggested to Herakles and Athena sounding disappointed. 'Maybe we're too late.'

Herakles said nothing.

'If the monster were already dead, we wouldn't have been sent here,' Athena explained to him.

'Do you intend to fight the monster?' Astron asked the group.

'I intend to kill it,' explained Herakles.

'I go swimming in the lake, and I've never been harmed. I have never even seen it. I think it is all just a big myth,' she explained to them.

'But you do know of it? You must have heard of the deaths and attacks and such?' Herakles asked.

'Oh, I've heard of it, but I assumed that it was just superstitious nonsense,' she answered.

'We'll just have to wait,' Athena concluded.

'I'd better go,' Astron decided. 'Good luck with your quest.'

'Thank you,' Iolaus replied clearly showing disappointment at her departure. 'She's really nice,' he added after she was out of ear shot.

Herakles scoffed. 'She's probably the monster that we've come to kill,' Herakles said teasingly.

'What?'

'The lioness was able to change into a woman, and I'll bet that the Hydra can also.'

Iolaus said nothing. He hoped that Herakles was wrong.

Herakles stretched his muscles and swung his sword arm. Both men then began to dress for battle. Iolaus had been kitted out by his uncle, and they both had a fine assortment of leather arm and leg protectors, and an array of razor-sharp weapons.

Athena stood up making to leave. 'I must do my privy,' she explained. 'Don't start the fight without me.' And she headed off to find a place to complete her toilet. As she walked around a large rock she almost walked into Hera. 'Hera!'

'Athena.'

'What! Why…?'

'I could ask the same of you,' Hera retorted.

'I'm here to protect, Herakles.'

'And I'm here to make certain he is defeated!'

'Why are you doing this? Why do you blame Herakles for Zeus's indiscretions?'

'Because I can, and I want to!' she smirked. 'One day Zeus will realise that he shouldn't betray our marriage!'

'This Hydra is none of your doing?' continued Athena. 'Why would you protect it?'

'The Hydra! I do not care whether it lives or it dies. All I want is for Herakles to die as a warning to all woman to stay away from my husband,' she explained. 'If the Hydra fails, I might just kill it myself as punishment.'

'What are you up to?'

'I've arranged a little support for the Hydra so it can defeat Herakles,' Hera explained.

'What kind of support?' Athena demanded.

'Meet Karkinos,' Hera turned and pointed to a giant crab that now scuttled sideways out of the lake and onto the land. It was bigger than the largest bull she had ever seen. Its two pincer claws were enormous and clearly razor sharp. It now snapped them open and shut as a precursor to battle. The giant crab moved past the women and advanced toward Herakles and Iolaus. Athena could only watch in horror as her two companions were attacked by the giant snapping claws of a crab monster. Caught unawares, the two men were driven into the lake in their hasty retreat from it.

As they were fending off its snapping claws, the Hydra slowly surfaced closely behind them. It screeched and breathed foul breath onto them. They were now at risk of becoming overcome from her toxic fumes. Herakles shouted to Iolaus to retreat farther but they both were busy fending off the crab from the shore side and the Hydra from the lake side. 'Cover your mouth!' Herakles shouted. 'The air is toxic.' They both moved their neck bands up to cover their mouths at the same time they were wielding their swords fending off the monster's attacks.

Hera laughed at the scene. To her, it seemed comical watching the two men fighting the beasts that were so obviously bigger and stronger than they were. Athena responded to her laughter by kicking Hera in the shins. Hera yelped in pain and surprise.

Herakles motioned for Iolaus to go farther out as Herakles swam the other way to the shore. He quickly climbed a massive rock and then launched himself onto the crab's back, his weight shattering the shell. Herakles then thrust his sword into the largest crack, instantly killing Karkinos. But his sword was now so firmly lodged into the beast, that Herakles could not retrieve it. He looked about desperately as he needed to aid Iolaus. Meanwhile, Iolaus had been lucky enough to cut off one of the Hydra's nine heads. The Hydra recoiled briefly in shock. Both men watched in amazement as the Hydra slowly grew two new heads in its place and was then able to continue its attack.

'Herakles, come here!' Athena summoned.

Herakles and Iolaus ran to Athena. She had unpacked the long box and now handed Herakles a long golden sword.

'Wow!' exclaimed Herakles.

'It is a gift from your father,' Athena explained.

'Zeus?'

'Yes, the one and only.'

'Err, that's all very touching,' Iolaus interrupted, 'But we're kind of in the middle of a battle,' he pointed toward the lake where the ten headed Hydra seemed to be patiently waiting to resume battle with them. Its screamed and its battle cries were deafening as it belched out smoke and flames.

'The Hydra can't fight you here on the land,' Athena explained. 'That's why Hera conjured the crab.'

'Hera?'

'Later,' recommended Athena. 'First you must deal with the Hydra. Use your new sword.'

'I will, thank you.'

'Your foot is bleeding,' Athena observed.

'I cut it when I landed on the crab's shell,' Herakles explained. 'It'll have to wait.'

'What are we to do about this head regrowing thing?' Iolaus asked in desperation.

Athena stood tall and issued instructions. 'Herakles, as you cut off the heads, Iolaus will use a flaming torch to cauterise the severed wounds. That should be binding enough to prevent new heads from growing.'

'Fire!' Herakles yelled to Iolaus. 'We need a fire!'

Iolaus got to work starting a fire as Herakles began his duel with the Hydra. They did not want it to swim away. Careful not to cut off any heads, Herakles was able to avoid being bitten or burnt whilst managing to stab the beast several times. The cuts and gashes were beginning to weaken the Hydra, but the fight also took its toll on Herakles who was also beginning to tire.

Iolaus was suddenly beside him. He held an enormous burning torch and nodded to his uncle that he was now ready to re-join the fight. As the Hydra lunged with one of its heads, Herakles swung his new golden sword up and cleanly sliced through its neck, severing the head from the body. Iolaus quickly thrust the flame into the open cut and the flesh sizzled and the wound sealed. The Hydra initially recoiled from the pain caused by the burn, but it soon attacked again but this time with two of its other heads. Herakles swung down and then up and both heads were decapitated and once again Iolaus burnt the flesh. The battle continued for a long time.

Athena watched in trepidation alongside Hera who joined her to watch in fascinated anticipation. Finally, the Hydra was in its death throws. All its heads were now decapitated, and the flesh cauterised. Eventually, as the Hydra lay dying in the shallows, a massive flock of enormous black feathered birds settled on its now headless body and started pecking at the open wounds.

'They must be the clean-up crew,' Herakles observed still panting from battle fatigue. Both exhausted men fell to the ground.

Athena now turned to Hera who had been mesmerised watching the battle. Hera now looked despondent at Herakles victory turned to see Athena advancing toward her. Clearly, she had not expected being tackled as so she stood passively and undefended as Athena drove her shoulder into Hera's stomach lifting her high in the air before they both fell crashing to the ground. Athena then repeatedly punched Hera hard in the face. They struggled but eventually Hera managed to push Athena off her. 'Athena!' she screamed. Athena briefly stopped and stared at Hera, but then forcibly slapped her face. 'Athena!' Hera screamed again. 'In Zeus's name, please stop hitting me!'

'You leave them alone!' Athena ordered.

'Okay, I will.' Hera conceded. She held up her hands in obeisance.

'From now on and for always,' continued Athena.

'Yes, yes, just don't hit me,' She answered. 'We're goddesses after all, let us behave like them.'

'Gods and goddesses are the worst!' Athena screamed in a rare burst of unrestrained anger. 'And right now, you are the worst of all of us!'

'I said I would leave them alone, what more do you want?'

'Remove Herakles's headaches!' Athena ordered.

'You seem to have that under control with your herbs and potions.'

'Get rid of them completely.'

'I will think about it.' But her scorn beguiled her face.

'I am curious. What promises did you make to that crab?' Herakles asked Hera indicating the crushed remains of the monster. 'How did you get it to attack us?'

'The crab thought I offered immortality through life,' Hera explained. 'I actually offered it immortality through legend, and a place in the stars.'

'What?' Athena was surprised. 'Why?'

'It looks dead to me,' Herakles concluded.

'I want its image to remain in the night sky to remind all woman to keep away from my husband. I want all women to remain faithful to their husbands. I am fed up with all the infidelity, as it will be the end of civilisation.'

'Then do it!' demanded Athena. 'Give this crab its own place in the heavens. Deliver you message. But make it such that men must be faithful to their wives also.'

Hera looked at her. Slowly she nodded her agreement.

Herakles and Iolaus watched alongside Athena as Hera lifted her arms high, with hands pointing at the heavens. 'I Hera, Queen of the Gods, cast the image of this crab into the heavens to commemorate the glory of...' she looked at Herakles and continued, 'Herakles's victory over it, thereby protecting the people and livestock of the town of Lerna. The crab' image is now also the reminder to all who are married, that they must remain faithful.'

Athena drew in a deep breath seemingly satisfied with Hera and the outcome.

The air was now very still and quiet. They turned to look at the remains of the Hydra and were surprised to see that all the birds that were previously hungrily eating its remains were all dead. 'The Hydra's blood must be poisonous,' Herakles concluded. He approached the dead beast and bent down toward it, carefully capturing some of its still draining blood into a secure vessel. When he was finished, he, Athena and Iolaus turned and walked away without uttering a single word to Hera.

Hera watched them leave. She then raised her arms to the heavens once more. 'I Hera, Queen of the Gods, cast the image of this Hydra into the heavens to commemorate the glory of Herakles battle and the Hydra's defeat.' The remains of the Hydra suddenly burst into flames and vanished in a cloud of thick black smoke.

A bruised and slightly indignant Hera sighed as she watched the Hydra burst into flames, and then she also vanished. She had instantly returned home to Mount Olympus.

Later that day, the three travellers set up their camp, ate, and rested.

At night, they lay relaxing under the stars, and they gazed at the night sky.

'Look Uncle!' Iolaus pointed to the night sky. Two new constellations had appeared that night for the first time. Both were symbolic of their recent victory and celebrated their bravery. "The Crab", that later came to be known as "Cancer", and "The Hydra" that kept that name.

***

The three heroes finally returned to the city, and once again the news of their victory had preceded them. Entertainers were performing a play with a giant of a man playing the part of Herakles and he was duelling with another performer dressed in a ridiculous crab costume. Farther along the road, singers loudly sang songs of praise, and there were many who yelled supportive chants for Herakles. They also chanted for Athena, and Iolaus who was delighted to hear praises about him. Iolaus attracted the eyes of many of the beautiful young women who were clearly enamoured of him. He flushed with embarrassment at this unexpected windfall. His uncle gave him a shoulder hug. 'You still have much to learn in that area,' he told him laughing.

'Oh, but Uncle, I'm so very willing to learn,' he replied grinning enthusiastically.

The king gave them a hearty welcome and the evening was spent at his palace feasting with a splendid banquet of food, much wine, loud music, and dancing.

The following morning the king told them of the rewards that Herakles had earned and then explained to him the details of his third labour. Iolaus at once showed his enthusiasm as Herakles accepted the task.

'I will not travel any more with you on your quests, Herakles,' Athena explained to him when they had returned to their palace chambers. 'I must spend some time here in the city and continue with my other duties.'

'I will miss you.' he told her.

'I'll celebrate each of your victories.' she assured him with a smile.

'I thank you for your confidence, your guidance and your assistance. I would not have succeeded so far without you.'

'Please, visit me again before you leave,' she invited.

'Yes of course,' Herakles agreed.

They embraced and then Athena gave Iolaus a hug also.

Iolaus looked at Athena and asked, 'Athena, Is Zeus your father?'

'He is,' she replied.

'Then you are Herakles half-sister?'

'That's correct,' she confirmed then looked puzzled at Herakles. 'But you already knew that?'

'I did. But I hope it wasn't the reason why you helped us.'

'I helped him because I could, and I believed it was the right thing to do.'

Herakles grabbed Iolaus in a playful headlock. 'You ask too many questions. You're embarrassing your aunt.'

They laughed.

Athena left to return to her own home in the city. Herakles found himself without her for the first time in a long time. Iolaus however, found himself a willing bed partner named Ania, and they settled in for the night.

Herakles was resolved to get a good night's sleep before their departure in the morning, when there was a knock on the door. He opened it to find two young women standing before him. They were smiling at him in eager anticipation. 'The king thought you might need a massage,' the first one explained. 'And we thought we might be the perfect girls for the job,' the other added giggling.

Herakles opened the door wider to let them in. Smiling at the girls as their clothes fell to the floor, Herakles was now resolved to enjoy this unexpected windfall. 'It's good to be the hero,' he murmured to himself.

The following morning the King summonsed Herakles into his chambers. He informed Herakles that despite the bravery and skills employed, he had decided that the task of defeating the Hydra was disallowed. He had received too much assistance from Iolaus and for him to succeed with completing his ten tasks, then he must do them solo. He was allowed to keep his reward for defeating the Hydra, but its defeat would not count toward his ten labours. Disappointed as he was, Herakles accepted the decision without argument or resentment.

Herakles explained to Iolaus the king's recent determination. He explained to Iolaus that he could not accompany him any longer, as he was meant to complete his tasks without any physical assistance. Iolaus took the news well. He and Ania had developed a strong bond and he was already planning to marry her. He had quickly decided that they would visit his parents, introduce his future bride to them, marry, and then they'd embark on their own adventures.

Herakles felt that this was a rushed decision, but he chose to say nothing. His own lack of success in relationships meant he now felt unqualified to comment.

In the morning, they met at Athena's place to say their farewells. They sadly parted company, but each promised that they would be reunited one day.

***

For his next task, Herakles was sent to capture the Ceryneian Hind named Cerynites. He was advised that it was swift and that it could outrun the speed of an arrow. He would recognise it by its golden antlers and bronzed hooves. He was warned that this doe was sacred to Artemis and that he must capture it unharmed.

Eventually Herakles captured Cerynites, but he inadvertently wounded it in the process. Herakles was startled when he was confronted by Artemis, who demanded an explanation. He managed somehow to skilfully lay the blame for the beast's injury onto King Eurystheus, and so he escaped Artemis' wrath. After presenting the beast to the king, he was instructed to return it to its natural habitat.

***

Herakles next mission was to destroy a monstrous boar that was ravaging the area around Mount Erymanthus. During this task, Herakles paid a visit to his old friend and mentor, a wise and kindly Centaur named Chiron. He was the tutor to many Greek heroes and Greek Prince's, in art, medicine, warfare, philosophy and astronomy. There he met some other visiting Centaurs, and they ended up in a dispute over the ownership of some wine. Several Centaurs died during the ensuing battle and Chiron was fatally wounded by inadvertently being wounded by an arrow that Herakles had loosed which was laced with the poisonous blood from the Hydra. The arrow had killed the intended target, but it continued through that centaur and into Chiron wounding him. Poor Chiron was fated to suffer terribly from the poison, and Herakles was now distressed for what had happened and that he was now powerless to help. Chiron begged Herakles to end his pain by ending his life and reluctantly Herakles tried but the wise tutor could not die as he was the immortal son of a Titan. Eventually, Chiron persuaded Herakles to resume his labours and made him promise to return to him when he could.

After leaving Chiron to his fate, Herakles decided to capture, but not to kill the boar. He took it back alive and released it inside the king's quarters as a joke. The king was so scared that he hid inside a bronze urn until his own men could kill the beast and rescue their king. Eurystheus chastised Herakles for his behaviour, but when Herakles explained about the imminent death of his dearest friend Chiron, the king became sympathetic and forgave him. He suggested that Herakles take some time off and have sea voyage before completing his remaining tasks.

He had recently learned that Jason was recruiting heroes for a sea voyage to liberate the Golden Fleece from a faraway land. Herakles immediately liked the idea of an ocean voyage and so he accepted the kings advise and took leave of his tasks to get some fresh air, adventure, and comradery. He was away for many months and experienced numerous adventures as an Argonaut. When he was inadvertently parted from the ships company after being betrayed by two of his shipmates, he returned to mainland Greece to resume his tasks.

***

Augeas was a son of Helios, and he had one of the largest cattle herds in the region. The smell from their dung was atrocious, and many of the king's subjects were constantly complaining that Augeas had a responsibility to clean it up and remove the odorous problem. Augeas was absent from his farm as he was still sailing with Jason on the Argo. His manager strongly argued that as they were the largest supplier of meat and milk for the area, he was therefore owed both respect and assistance with the clean-up task. So, when Herakles returned home from sailing with Jason and the crew of the Argos, he was immediately given the unpleasant task.

King Eurystheus was clearly displeased that Herakles had been away for so long, and had decided that Herakles alone should clean up the accumulated dung from the cattle stables as his punishment.

As a joke, the king told him that he must rid the stables of all its dung in one day. Herakles being unaware of the enormity of the task accepted it willingly. When he arrived at the stables, he observed that the river Alpheus flowed nearby. It was in full flow after a heavy winter rains. He examined the banks of the river and calculated that if he dislodged an enormous giant rock high above the rivers path, that it would create a dam that it would divert the flow of water through the stables. It took him three hours of hard work digging to undermine the rock, but the boulder was eventually freed and it rolled noisily down the hill and exactly into position. The water immediately poured over the river banks and temporarily flowed through the stables. All the dung was washed cleanly away. The stench was atrocious, but later the landholders downstream would remark about how much more productive their soil was, and that they learned of the effectiveness of spreading manure onto paddocks to improve the yield of the harvest.

Soon the Alpheus River had cut a new path around the boulder and its strong current resumed flowing along its normal course. The stables were clean and the smell was once more bearable. Augeas's farm now had an additional industry of supplying manure. The king was praised by his people, and Herakles was praised by the king and suitably rewarded for his ingenuity and hard work.

***

Herakles next labour was to visit Lake Stymphalian in the region of Acadia. There, the birds were preying on humans, killing and eating many of them. The birds were colossal predators and they had enormous wings, and their beaks and claws were as hard as iron. When perched, they were able to blend perfectly into their environment and they were exceptionally difficult to find. In this way, they were able to avoid previous attempts to hunt them. Herakles still wore the pelt of the Nemean Lioness, and this offered him some protection from their claws. Armed with a long bow and numerous lethal arrows, he ventured into their killing fields. At first, he could not see them, but by clashing giant bronze castanets that he had brought with him for this purpose, he frightened the birds into taking flight. As they did, they became visible and Herakles was able to let loose his arrows to bring them all down. They were now dead and Herakles had completed another task.

***

For his next challenge, Herakles was ordered to capture a giant bull on the island of Crete. The bull was enormous and resented human contact. It constantly harassed the dairy herd and milk production had effectively stopped. Herakles tied a long rope to a giant tree. He formed a lasso with its other end and approached the Cretan Bull. He managed to drop the lasso onto the bull's horns and then run away. As the bull chased him the lasso slip knot tightened and the bull was secure. Herakles headed clockwise around the tree with the bull keeping pace. The more circuits they walked around the tree the shorter the rope became. Soon the bull was hard up against the tree and had stepped inside another lasso that Herakles had previously laid out at the base of the tree. Herakles pulled on the rope capturing the beast by its front legs and he tied it secure. He later presented the bull as his gift to the local people of Tiryn. There were many well fed happy people that night, and Herakles stayed with them to join in the celebrations as an honoured hero.

***

King Eurystheus was so consistently praised by his people for managing Herakles so well, that he was feeling delightfully positive when assigning more near impossible tasks to his hero. He next ordered Herakles to deal with a Thracian named Diomedes. He had a herd of wild mares who were fed a diet of human flesh. Diomedes disposed of his enemies remains in this fashion, but the horses were now becoming a serious problem and were attacking people who passed near his home. Even when Diomedes was at peace, the roaming horses who had a taste for human flesh sought them out, killing and eating them. When Herakles paid a visit to Diomedes, he refused point blank to stop the carnage. So, Herakles punched him until he was unconscious, and then tied him to wooden stakes spread out on the ground. He woke him up by splashing water onto his face and then proceeded to cut him in several places. The mares immediately smelt the blood, became inflamed with blood lust, and then attacked and gored their owner. After the feast was over, Herakles herded the mares into a well fenced paddock that had lush green pasture. He forced them through hunger to resume a traditional diet of hay and oats. At first the mares resented their confinement, but over time and with much loving patience, he was eventually able to tame the mares and even ride them. For the duration Diomede's home became his own.

When the locals learned of Diomedes fate, they came visiting Herakles, bringing him gifts and singing his praises. Many people encouraged him to take up permanent residence. Eventually the mares were ready and so he herded them all to Eurystheus and presented them as his gift. He was generously rewarded, but given no time to relax as he was immediately set his next task.

***

Living just east of Greece, there was a fierce tribe of warlike warrior women who were known as the Amazons. They had a reputation for plundering Greek communities for their weapons and food. They didn't grow any of their own crops or make clothes or tools, preferring to steal them instead. They held a small group of male prisoners and they treated them as slaves, but often used them for carnal pleasure and for breeding. Dissenters were publicly killed and they were quickly replaced. The female babies were raised and taught the Amazonian ways. Male babies however, were either immediately killed, or they were abandoned in the woods to die a death from predators, or a slow death from exposure to the harsh elements. The local Greeks feared them and wanted them to be dealt with decisively, and permanently.

Eurystheus realised that even Herakles could not defeat them on his own, but he did command Herakles to perform a difficult task against their current queen. Her name was Hippolyte and she possessed a beautiful jewel encrusted golden girdle. Its reputation was well known almost as much as the reputation of the fierce behaviour of the Amazonian women. Eurystheus's daughter Admete's, vividly dreamt that she would one day own that girdle, and so she continually pestered her father to obtain it for her. Eurystheus didn't like to disappoint his daughter and so he ordered Herakles to obtain the girdle by any means necessary. He journeyed for many days before reaching the region controlled by the Amazons.

Herakles quickly realised that there were far too many of them for him to defeat. He decided he had to hide during the day, and he only proceeded closer to their base during night-time. He eventually learned the location of Hippolyte's home and remained hidden in the trees near to their encampment, as he watched them and learned their routines. He saw the male slaves being locked away at night-time and decided that if he released them, then in the confusion of their escape, he could locate and hopefully, steal the girdle.

Under a quarter moon, on a cool cloudless night, Herakles stealthily entered the Amazon's encampment. The male slave quarters were secured, but unguarded. Herakles gathered weapons from a rack and then took them to the door of the slave's confinement. Using a long steel pole, he prised open the door and went inside. He shook awake the slaves and told them he had come to liberate them. He was amazed when some of them told him that they didn't want to leave, but many of the newer arrivals did. He led them outside, armed them, and pointed out their escape route. As they fled, Herakles went back into hiding and watched. The escapees were as noisy as Herakles had predicted. Soon the alarm was raised, and the women awoke, realised what was happening, and gave chase after their slaves. They were screaming and enraged that they were escaping.

Queen Hippolyte remained in the encampment and directed her warriors into the chase. She was wearing night wear but she was without her legendary girdle. Herakles took advantage of her absence to sneak into her sleeping quarters. There he located the girdle which was proudly displayed on a rack constructed for that purpose. He placed his sword onto the floor, and was about to liberate the girdle from its fastenings, when he was startled by Hippolyte. She may have been without her girdle, but she did have her sword. Angry at Herakles presence, she advanced aggressively toward him. Herakles was caught off guard, but in a flash of inspiration, he smiled generously as he casually disrobed and lay backwards on her bed. Hippolyte stopped and stared at him, she shrugged as she assumed it was his willingness to submit to her as her sex slave that had brought him here, so she too discarded her sword and shed her clothes and proceeded to mount him. As she did, Herakles reached up caressing her body until he eventually reached her throat and held it firmly. He then slowly squeezed the life out of her. She grasped at his massive wrist, but she was unable to break free, or summon help.

It only took Herakles a few moments to choke the life out of the Amazon Queen. When he knew that she was dead, he lowered her gently to the bed and kissed her forehead. He dressed and left the room with the girdle now packed in a bag which he slung over his shoulder. He had to kill a few Amazonian warriors as he fled the area, but he was soon in the clear. For a while he only travelled at night, but later when he was far away from Amazon territory, he travelled during the daylight.

The king's daughter, Admete's was delighted with the girdle. The king instructed Herakles to promise that if asked by his daughter, that the Queen of the Amazon's had happily gifted it to her when she was learned of his darling princess's prophecy.

***

King Eurystheus next ordered Herakles to the far west of Greece to a land that was the furthest point that any Greek person had previously travelled. He had to sail across a body of water that was known as the Mediterranean. The sea was nearly pinched shut at its far western end, with only a thin stretch of water separating the two headlands. Beyond that it opened into the as yet uncharted Atlantic Ocean.

Herakles had to journey a great distance to obtain cattle from Geryon, a three-bodied monster of a man, and his giant herdsman named Eurtion. They also had a ferocious two headed dog named Orthrus who helped them guard the herd. Orthrus was the second child of Echidna and Typhon. Some say Herakles hitched a ride with Helios in his giant cup as he travelled from east to west. Others say he sailed by ship and returned the same way with the cattle. Either way, Herakles completed the task with a bit of help from the locals. They feared

Geryon and many claimed that he and Eurtion regularly stole cattle from them to increase the size of their own herd. Herakles sailed to the red island of Eytheir where he managed to defeat Geryon and Eurtion by shooting a single massive arrow through the two of them as they raced in single file toward him. He then dispassionately slew Orthrus and their other savage dogs with the sword gifted to him by Zeus. The locals were grateful and so they named the two flanking rocky peaks on either side of the straight as the "The Pillars of Herakles" in his honour.

On his way home he was attacked by thieves who were intent on liberating some of the cattle from him. Their numbers were so great that Herakles ran out of arrows and was almost overwhelmed, when suddenly an unexplained shower of rocks and large stones fell from the sky, killing all the attackers. He never learned the identity of his rescuer.

***

When Herakles finally reached Eurystheus and delivered the remaining cattle, he confronted the king. 'King Eurystheus, I have slain the Lioness that terrorised the people of Nemea, destroyed the Hydra of Lake Lerna, and I captured Artemis's Hind. I have brought you the boar from Mount Erymanthus, and I have washed the dung away from your friend's stables. I have killed the demon birds at Lake Stymphalian, and I have dispatched the Cretan Bull. I tamed the wild mares of Diomedes and I brought you the girdle that belonged to the Queen of the Amazonians. Now, I have delivered the cattle of Geryon to you. These are my ten completed tasks that I have now carried out for you at great personal risk. I now bid you, that in your good will and with all your previous assurances, that I humbly request that I be paid my deserved dues, and that I be released from your service.' Herakles proclaimed and bowed gracefully.

'Herakles you have served me well and risked your life many times. You have many battle scars, and the legends of your great feats are well known across all of Greece. The stories of your ingenuity and your magnificent victories are by far the most popular of all our Greek heroes. I am grateful for your deeds, and I accept that they have benefited me, my family, and the people of Tiryn greatly. However, I have counted only eight deeds properly executed in my service, so you still have two more to complete.'

As Eurystheus delivered the news he examined the massive man's face seeking a clue as to his reaction. Would he capitulate and do two more, or would he abandon the agreed labours and walk away from the promised rewards, or would he dispute his conclusion and become angry?

'I counted ten,' Herakles said looking doubtful. 'I now recall that you disallowed the killing of the Hydra of Lake Lerna because my nephew, Iolaus assisted me, and I accepted that the completion the tasks were for me alone. Okay, Because of Iolaus assistance, I agree I owe you one more task.' Herakles smiled hoping that they had reached a new agreement.

Eurystheus remained steadfast. 'Do two more deeds and then you are completed. I have also disallowed the cleaning of the stables as it was too easily carried out. Repositioning a rock was inspired, but cleaning dung was a task unworthy of the mighty Herakles, and I regret asking you to do it. You should demand that it be struck from the record of your exploits.' Eurystheus let his opinion hang heavily in the air.

Herakles stood still and said nothing. He too had considered the stables to be an unworthy task, and he was pleased when the giant boulder presented itself as an easy solution to an otherwise disgusting task. Diverting the river was funny, but in truth he agreed that it was not a feat worth bragging about. At the time he felt cleaning the dung was punishment for releasing the boar in the king's chambers. It was perhaps prudent not to risk antagonising the king over that labour and so he decided to capitulate and do the two more labours. 'I will do as you ask.'

***

Eurystheus had learned about a giant apple tree that was a gift to Hera by her grandmother Gaia on her wedding day. This tree grew golden apples. Even Eurystheus accepted that removing the tree would be an insult to both Gaia and Hera, and he did not want to risk Herakles or harming the tree. The apples it grew however, were its replenishing bounty, and picking some would not harm the tree. He charged Herakles with the task of finding the tree, picking its fruit, and then returning home with a basket of golden apples.

Herakles set off the following day to find a sea god named Nereus. He was known for the bounty of the sea's harvest and as such he was favoured by all fishermen. Many called him "the old man of the sea," and it was said that he was wise and that his powers as a seer were great. Herakles hoped Nereus would help him find the golden apple tree.

Herakles spotted the god out to sea. He took a small boat and rowed the short distance to the oracles fishing boat. When he boarded, he found the old god struggling to bring up a net filled with fish. Herakles smiled watching him strain. Being skilled at catching fish was one thing, but you also needed the strength to bring in the heavy haul, and land it on board the vessel. Herakles reached over and single handed, he pulled the net up and laid it onto the deck. He then helped Nereus secure the fish in boxes as they talked.

'I know you didn't row out to me just to assist me with my catch,' Nereus stated after they had dealt with inconsequential pleasantries.

'You are truly a powerful seer,' Herakles smiled.

'I'm not you know,' Nereus smiled. 'If I were, I would have known that you were coming to visit me, and the nature of your purpose for doing so.'

'And I would say that you did know, and that you caught so many fish with the full foresight that I'd be there to assist you,' Herakles replied and Nereus burst into laughter with Herakles quickly joining in. They at once liked each other.

'How can I, a humble fisherman, assist a hero of Greece?'

'I'm charged with the task of finding a fruit tree that belongs to Hera that bears golden apples.' Herakles looked at the old man hoping for some glimmer that he knew what he was talking about, and that he'd be willing to assist him.

'Hera's golden apple tree,' Nereus said nodding knowingly. 'Eurystheus must really like you. He's sending you to pluck fruit from the tree owned by the very woman who cursed you.'

'The irony has not escaped me,' Herakles snorted.

'The tree you seek is in the centre of a magnificent garden and it is cared for by many nymphs. They are known as the Hesperides. They were chosen for the task as they are associated with rain and warm sunshine, and they can keep Hera's Garden lush, green, and healthy all through the year. The golden apple tree grows in a garden which is on Mount Atlas where the Titan Atlas is charged with the responsibility of holding the sky up above our heads. As well as looking after the garden, the nymphs feed and attend Atlas, as he can't escape from his task. I suggest you befriend Atlas and arrange for him to pick the fruit for you, and then you'll return home with your apples without having offended Hera personally.' He studied Herakles face before continuing. He nodded knowingly. 'You will also encounter a dragon who is charged with guarding the tree. When resting under the warmth of Helios, the dragon is small and he has only one tiny head. When it becomes alarmed, it grows enormously and sprouts numerous enlarged heads all with huge mouths filled with razor sharp teeth. You must destroy it without it seeing or sensing you. If you don't, its hide will grow too thick for your sword, or arrows, or spears to penetrate. This dragon might kill you, Herakles.' Nereus words hung heavily in the air.

The plan seemed simple enough. Herakles and Nereus drank wine and they spent much of the evening talking through the details. Later they feasted on some fish that Nereus had prepared. Looking up at the night sky, Nereus pointed out the constellation of the Dragon that Zeus had placed in the skies to appease Hera. He then guided Herakles eyes to a cluster of stars within the constellation and explained. 'Those stars represent the Hesperides who tend to Hera's Garden. Zeus honoured them to appease Hera after she confronted him about his attempted seduction of Europa.'

Eventually they slept, and at dawn of the following day, Herakles bade his farewell and set off for Mount Atlas.

***

On route to retrieve the Golden Apples, Herakles came across a bizarre sight. He found the Titan, Prometheus chained to a rock-strewn cliff face. Whilst he appeared to be in good health, he had fear written all over his face.

'Are you, Prometheus?' Herakles asked as he stood before the bewildered Titan.

'I am. And you are?' Prometheus asked.

'I am Herakles, son of Zeus and I...' Herakles began to explain.

'I have heard of you,' Prometheus cut him off and looked anxiously into the sky.

'What do you fear?' Herakles was concerned. He knew much of this Titan as he was reputed to be the founder of human kind. As a benevolent Titan, he had sought to enrich human capacity to learn and to fend for themselves. For those in the know, Prometheus was a force for championing human development and self-sufficiency, but he hadn't been seen, or heard about, for a very long time.

'Zeus punished me for my gift of fire to the humans so that they could cook meat. I have been bound to this cliff by these chains for thirteen human generations.'

'Seems harsh.'

'It was my defiance that angered him. He did not care about the fire.'

Herakles examined the chain. 'You seem strong enough to break these chains,' Herakles concluded. 'Perhaps if we both pulled on them, then maybe our combined strength will break you free.'

'You are kind and you're correct. I alone cannot break these chains, even when I'm at full strength. They are made from Adamantine steel, the strongest ever forged. Each day before I can fully recover, an eagle also arranged by Zeus, swoops down and attacks me and rips out my liver...' Prometheus started to explain.

'Your liver!' Herakles was shocked. 'Just for helping humans and giving them power over fire?'

'That is the crux of it. Soon the eagle will return to attack me and disable me once more.' Prometheus clearly did not enjoy this ritual.

'I will kill this eagle for you and set you free,' Herakles offered.

'My nemesis is huge, powerful, and intelligent. It will not be possible to kill it whilst the eagle is in flight,' Prometheus advised. 'Besides, Zeus will not permit it.' Prometheus hung his head low, clearly resigned to his fate.

'My friend, Chiron wants to die. He is a Titan like yourself, so he too is immortal. He was accidentally wounded by my poison tipped arrow and he is now in constant pain.' Herakles explained to Prometheus. 'He asked me to end his life, but at the time I was unable to do so. I will now ask my father to do this for me and also to release you from your torment.' Herakles felt Prometheus studying the sincerity in his face. Herakles called up to the skies. 'Father, Zeus, king of all the gods, if ever you have heard my call, listen to me now and answer my plea!'

Zeus instantly appeared before Herakles. 'What do you want?' He asked and then looked at Prometheus and laughed. 'Do you want my forgiveness for this traitor?' He laughed some more.

'Actually, I want you to end the pain and suffering of my friend Chiron, and then to allow me to release Prometheus,' Herakles explained.

'But the eagle enjoys his daily feast of fresh liver,' Zeus countered. 'What would the eagle do if I released him?'

'The eagle wouldn't care if the eagle were dead,' Herakles explained.

'The eagle is far too wise and swift even for your arrow, my son.' Just then the sky filled with the shrieks of the mighty predator. It flew in ever descending downward spirals getting closer to Prometheus for its ritual attack and feed.

'And if you are wrong?' Herakles challenged above the noise of the bird.

'Then I will do as you ask, and I will end Chiron's pain by ending his life.'

'And you will allow me to release Prometheus?' Herakles added. 'It should be an easy request for you to grant me, as you already believe that I will fail,' he explained, and his smile taunted his father.

Zeus smiled. 'Very well,' he agreed as he nodded. This he had to see.

Herakles got closer to Prometheus and explained his plan. 'I will hide, and when the eagle lands on your body, grab onto its talons and hold them tight. I will shoot an arrow through the eagle's heart and that'll put an end to your torment.'

Prometheus studied him and then nodded his gratitude.

Herakles hid behind some large boulders and soon enough the eagle descended once more onto Prometheus. The Titan grabbed the claws of the mighty bird and Herakles stepped out of hiding and drew back on the giant bow, let loose the arrow straight through the eagles' heart. The eagle died instantly and fell to the ground. Then, with their joint strength, the two men were able to break the chains. Prometheus was freed. Zeus had watched the events unfold and vanished as soon as they were over. Prometheus hugged Herakles in gratitude. He was eager to return to his family and resume his life helping humans.

Later, Herakles had a vision of Zeus with Chiron who was now deceased. He was pleased that his father had honoured their arrangement but remained saddened by the unfortunate accident that led to his demise.

Later that night, a new constellation known as Aquila appeared in the night sky. Zeus commemorated the Eagle for its services, and to serve as a reminder to Prometheus of his powers and complete rule over those in his domain.

***

It took Herakles many weeks to journey to the place of the golden apple tree. He sailed by small boat to the island and then climbed its only mountain to find Atlas arched under the weight of the sky. He seemed pleased to see Herakles, and he gave him a cheery wave in greeting. 'You must be Herakles,' The Titan god concluded. 'I have been told much about you and your ongoing exploits, and I had hoped that one day you'd visit me.' Atlas was clearly pleased with Herakles arrival.

Herakles laughed. 'It's a small world. An incestuous world and there are no secrets. I believe we are distant cousins of a sort.' He then winced at seeing Atlas burdened with holding up the sky. Even though air is light, the sheer volume of it weighed heavily on the burdened Titan.

'Why do you have such a burden?' Herakles asked.

'I chose the losing side when my family went to war. This is my punishment.'

'It is a heavy burden.'

'Would you like to carry this for me please, cousin? Just for a short time, whilst I stretch my legs?' Atlas asked trying hard to make his request seem innocent. He had long hoped to pass on his task to any man of Herakles reputed strength and courage. Maybe this was his opportunity.

Herakles winced. 'I'm actually in a bit of a bind myself. My master has bid me to fetch apples from Hera's golden apple tree, but it is guarded by nymphs who will resent my intrusion and they'll interfere with my task,' Herakles explained calmly hoping to strike a deal with the old Titan.

'I would offer to fetch some for you, but I have two problems.' Atlas played along hoping to win from the exchange. 'Firstly, the apple tree, whilst tended to by beautiful nymphs, it is also guarded by a multi-headed dragon, one sired by Typhon and Echidna. I have it on good authority that the dragon will kill me if I disturb the fruit.'

'I suppose the second is that you're a bit too busy holding up the sky, to be able to go and fetch the apples for me?' Herakles concluded.

'There is that,' Atlas agreed as he shifted the weight a little to make himself more comfortable.

'How about I first kill the dragon and then return here to you and hold up the sky whilst you stretch your legs and meet with the nymphs and pick the fruit. When you are ready you can bring me the basket full of apples.

'I have no love for that dragon. He savagely bit my daughter Maia when she returned home from attending Artemis. She suffered terribly from the wound, and sadly, I had to end her life.'

'A tragedy,' agreed Herakles.

'How will you kill the dragon?' Atlas asked, but he nodded his understanding when Herakles held up his giant bow. He then cautioned his co-conspirator. 'The dragon grows both in size and in the number of heads when he is alarmed. It would be best to kill him when he is resting.'

'Thanks for the advice,' Herakles said as he bowed and headed off to kill the dragon. He was soon perched near the top of a tall tree adjoining the gardens that surrounded the golden apple tree. He surveyed the scene. Several young women in silky breezy dresses busied themselves with the gardens, planting, feeding, weeding, and watering. Herakles marvelled at their elegance and beauty, and he remembered that it had been a long time since he'd lain with a woman. He also longed for a quieter time when he too could attend a garden and work a farm that was his, and perhaps even have a family of his own once more. Then the dragon came into view. The dragon was smaller than Herakles had imagined, but its current size was a poor indication of its skill and ferocity. The dragon seemed comfortable and relaxed contentedly amongst the busy Hesperides.

Herakles knocked his long bow with an arrow tipped with Hydra blood. Before drawing back on the bow, he felt the wind to allow for its speed and direction. The gentle breeze fell suddenly still as if it held its breath in anticipation of what was about to happen. Herakles took this cue and propelled the arrow through the garden air and into the forehead of the resting dragon. The full length of the arrow penetrated the dragon's skull with not even the arrows plumes showing. The piercing of the arrow, and the poison it carried, were instantaneous in its effect and the dragon died without reaction. The nearby nymphs were oblivious to the dragon's fate, content that he was sleeping peacefully.

Herakles then climbed down the tree and returned to Atlas. Wordlessly the giant Titan passed his load to Herakles. Atlas nodded his thanks, stretched, and then headed toward the garden. He later returned with a basket filled with golden apples and placed them at Herakles feet. 'I have one other small task to perform before I can resume my burden,' he explained to Herakles with a grin. 'I appreciate that you'll support the sky for me a little longer whilst I see to it?' He asked, clearly having no intention of ever returning.

'Of course, cousin.' Herakles capitulated gracefully. 'I'm only too happy to assist you further as you have given me good advice about the dragon, and you have fetched the golden apples for me. But before you go, could you pass me my bow and arrows, so that I may defend my new treasure during your absence?' Herakles indicated toward the now vulnerable basket with its precious prize. Atlas shrugged and passed Herakles his weapon. 'Could you also fetch me a cushion that I may place between my head and the sky, you see, I am unaccustomed to the weight and it is hurting my skull.' Atlas nodded his agreement and swiftly obtained a cushion and Herakles indicated his need for assistance in getting it into place so as to be comfortable. As the weight of the sky was transferred back to Atlas, Herakles ducked out from under it and was now free from its burden. Herakles quickly nocked an arrow into his bow and drew back on the weapon. He aimed it directly at Atlas. 'This arrow has the same poisonous blood on its tip that I used to kill the dragon. If you don't willingly resume your duties as assigned to you by our father, then you'll die.'

Atlas laughed. He immediately got comfortable as he resumed his stance, the sky once again firmly held into place by the massive Titan.

As Herakles departed, the basket held under his arm, he reflected on when he held the sky for Atlas, that he'd felt no weight of it at all. He posed as if he did, but was in reality, totally unburdened. Zeus it seems, had tricked Atlas into believing that he had this duty, but in truth, he could leave it any time, and no one would ever suffer from the sky falling on their heads.

As soon as Herakles completed his delivery of the golden apples to King Eurystheus, he was given no time to rest or luxuriate, as he was ordered to enter Hades and return with the three headed dog named Cerberus. King Eurystheus had believed that with the task of retrieving the golden apples that Herakles would fail, and he was pleasantly surprised when he had returned with them. As soon as Herakles had departed, the king sent riders carrying the golden apples with orders to quickly return them to the Hesperides with his profound apologies, as he now feared retribution from Hera. As for Herakles, maybe he'd be lucky, and Hades would keep him.

***

Herakles was mortal so for him to enter Hades' realm he needed to die, but to complete the task he needed to live. Herakles consulted an apothecary who gave him a potion that would render him dead enough to die, but not dead enough to stay dead. He would have one full day to complete his task or if he were still in Hades, he would remain dead. Herakles drank the potion and lay down. His heartbeat was now imperceptible, and he appeared dead. As he was the son of Zeus, he was rushed through to the underworld to meet his uncle. Hades was suitably impressed with his nephew's courage to enter his domain. Herakles explained his need to borrow Cerberus in order to complete his labours, and to free himself from Hera's wrath and misery. Hades sympathised, as he never liked his sister Hera, and agreed that Herakles could take his dog as long as Cerberus came to no harm and that he was quickly returned.

Hades warned that the dog, when angered, would not hesitate to attack him with its razor-sharp teeth, and that it could breathe out fire, and that it could even sprout snake heads all with lethal venom. Hades then insisted that Herakles use no weapons to capture or contain his favourite guard dog. Herakles agreed, but became initially daunted when confronted by the three headed beast. He then contrived a plan. He still wore the pelt of Zosma the Nemean Lioness that he had killed on his first labour. Herakles removed it from his shoulders and held the pelt before the three headed dog. Instantly the beast smelt the pelt, it reminded him of his mother and father, Echidna and Typhon. Zosma was his sister and the normally ferocious beast now whimpered with loss and grief. He now sadly missed his family. Herakles seized the opportunity to gently wrap the dog within Zosma's pelt. Hades was so impressed he allowed Herakles to immediately leave. As soon as Eurystheus sighted the three headed dog, he ordered it be returned to Hades. Herakles did so gladly, and he returned Cerberus all within the one day that the effects of the potion had allowed.

***

It was on a fine sunny day when Herakles came across is nephew Iolaus. He and Ania were now married and they lived on a small farm. The three sat together talking about the challenges they had each performed. Iolaus was reluctant to speak of his own victories as they were modest by Herakles accomplishments. As they spoke and drank, Herakles appetite turned to thoughts of food. Ania fetched bowls of cooked vegetables and bread that was starchy and tough to break into bit sized pieces. He didn't want to offend his hosts and so ate in silence.

When Ania cleared the table, Iolaus apologised to his uncle. 'She can't cook,' he lamented. She has no control over the farm animals and she won't butcher any of them for us to eat.' He looked despondent. 'I get paid to perform dangerous tasks, and I return home to soggy vegetables and stale bread.'

'You deserve better,' Herakles said without malice.

***

As Herakles had now completed twelve tasks, King Eurystheus kept his word and rewarded him with an enormous area of land. It was by a river that flowed throughout the year and its soil was fertile. Herakles the hero was able to return to farming once more. The wealth he had accumulated from his rewards was also doubled by the king as promised. Herakles now had enough money to build a farmhouse with sheds and fencing and plenty of livestock of chickens, ducks, geese, sheep and cattle. He was also able to hire labourers to work with him. His greatest happiness came from his loving bride, Deianeira. She bore him children and together they lived in peace and prosperity for a long time.

Herakles was often propositioned to go on quests and conquests as the stories of his legendary exploits continued to grow. At first, he resisted preferring the home life, but as their funds diminished and he grew more and more restless, he would temporarily depart from his farm in search of glory and more importantly for bounty. Sometimes his travels were over in weeks, but some took him away for many months. Each time he returned home to Deianeira, she would shower him with her love and made plans to take good care of him, hoping that he would stay home for good this time.

But it was on his final expedition that Herakles met and fell in love with Iole, a beautiful young princess of Oechalia. She was being held against her will, for refusing to marry the man her father had chosen for her. Herakles met her in the palace gardens quite unintentionally, but the love they felt for each other was as strong as it was instant.

She told him that her father had agreed that if any man of her choosing could best him in an archery challenge, that he would agree to her marrying the victor. Herakles loved a challenge. He was an expert with the bow and presented himself as a suitor for Iole's hand in marriage. Under the terms of Eurytus's agreement with his daughter, he accepted the contest.

Herakles achieved a perfect score and was victorious and so claimed Iole as his bride. Eurytus didn't know that Herakles was already married, but he did know that Herakles had killed his first wife Megara, when he had been driven mad by Hera. Herakles defended himself and explained that it was all in the past, and that Hera's curse was about to be lifted as he had completed the assigned tasks. Besides, the apothecary's remedy continued to work.

Eurytus remained unconvinced and so he refused their wedding. He explained to Iole that he feared for her safety, and that she should remain with her family. Iole was angry and ordered Herakles to rescue her and to take her away from this place. He willingly promised to help her escape her misery, and take her to his home to be his new wife. Her rescue turned disastrous when they were confronted by her family who were outraged by Herakles motives and they battled ferociously. Herakles first slayed Eurytus and then her three brothers. Many guards were also killed by Herakles sword. He almost destroyed the entire settlement as many of the buildings caught fire during the fighting.

As they journey to where Herakles lived, Iole announced her decision to leave him. He was bereft and dismayed, as he had killed many people to liberate her from her controlling family. Iole confessed that she had used him only for the purposes of being free of her father. She now planned to continue her life without Herakles. At first, he pleaded with her, but eventually he resorted to binding her to him, convinced that she would eventually come to love him and want to be his future bride.

***

When Herakles returned to his home, he now only wanted to be with Iole. He fully intended to explain to Deianeira about his true love for this new younger woman, and he desperately hoped that she would understand. But when he got there, he discovered that his home was under siege from a savage Centaur named Nessus. Nessus had killed many of his servants and farm hands and was now pursuing Deianeira through their home with the intention of raping her. Herakles entered his home, cornered, and stabbed the Centaur and saved Deianeira. She rushed into her husband's arms, grateful for being saved and overjoyed that he was home, but her joy turned quickly to confusion when Iole entered the room.

Even as the Centaur laid dying, Herakles felt the need to explain to Deianeira about his new found love for Iole. Deianeira burst into hysterical tears and fled the room. Iole felt embarrassed and so she went outside. Herakles was torn between comforting his wife and with being with Iole. He chose to follow Iole and reassured her that he would gently explain the strength of their love to Deianeira and make her understand. He promised her to make things right for their future together.

Meanwhile, Deianeira was getting angrier and was preparing to confront Herakles for his betrayal. As she searched the kitchen to find a suitable weapon, the dying Centaur spoke to Deianeira in sooth-ing words and told her that if she wanted to keep Herakles's love, she must give Herakles this potion that he was proffering toward her. In desperation, she took the potion and poured it into a cup. Herakles entered the room. He ignored the dying Centaur as he approached his wife who turned and offered him a drink which he innocently ac-cepted. He downed the liquid in a single gulp as he was desperate to explain himself to his wife, but the power of the poison was quick to take effect.

At first, Deianeira was delighted when she saw Herakles sway. She was convinced that Herakles was coming to his senses, and that his love for her was returning, but Herakles suddenly fell to the floor. Horrified, and in full concern she rushed to him only to discover that Herakles was dead. Deianeira next turned to Nessus accusingly, but the Centaur simply laughed loudly and claimed. 'Death to Her-akles, vengeance is mine for the grief I've suffered for my family killed by his sword on the slopes of Mount Pelion.' He then vio-lently coughed twice, clearly racked with pain, and then he also died. Deianeira grabbed the flask and drank the remaining poison know-ing her fate. The poison quickly took control, and then she too fell to floor, dead. Her body was now lying between her husband and the centaur. Iole, in her concern, entered the room. She saw the bodies, became alarmed, fled the room, and was never heard of again.

The servants discovered the bodies, and a period of mourning be-gan. Notices of Herakles death was sent out with messengers. Their son, Hyllus built a giant funeral pyre on the top of Mount Oeta. The funeral was attended by many thousands of people. They had come to say their farewell to the greatest living legend of the land. Iolaus was there also with his family and his two cousins Orpheus and Sisyphus, Herakles children from his first marriage. Herakles had never learned of their survival, despite the brother's intentions to one day visit with their father, but now it was too late.

King Eurystheus attended with his family and his ever-increasing retinue. He owed much of his prosperity to Herakles, and he was greatly saddened by his death. Athena was there also. She was as young and beautiful looking as ever, and she stood next to a hooded man. They were well back from the proceedings.

Philoctetes was given the task of lighting the fire. He was the beneficiary of Herakles bow and arrows, and he considered it a great honour to be asked to commit this great man to the afterlife. As the fire took hold, the hooded man wove his way through the crowd. To their astonishment, the man casually walked into the flames. Many saw it as a symbol of his grief and believed that the hooded man would choose to die to be with his hero in the afterlife. Their gasps and screeches soon turned to cheers and the flames consumed them both. Athena said and did nothing.

***

The heat and the smoke carried the souls of both Herakles and the hooded man up high in the sky. As they cooled, they descended, and Herakles realised that they had arrived near the top of a mountain. The man spoke to him for the first time.

'Welcome, Herakles. Welcome to your new home on Mount Olympus,' the man explained.

Herakles was stunned.

'Have you nothing to say?'

'But... I'm dead,' he stammered.

'Not any more the man explained. You have been granted immortality by the gods... well by me actually.'

'You?!'

'Yes,' replied the hooded man.

'Are you...?'

'Yes!' he answered, grinning while removing his hood. Zeus reached out and hugged his son. Herakles wept, but he said nothing.

It took some time for Herakles to adjust to being an immortal living with the gods and goddesses at Mount Olympus. At first, he just wandered about appreciating that everyone was friendly and welcoming. They all knew who he was, and they seemed overly familiar with his exploits. He met and fell in love with Hebe, the daughter of Zeus and Hera, the goddess of youth and his half-sister. He thought her a bit young at first, but she captivated his soul and he was ecstatic to be with her. It was with her that he realised that his headaches were gone as he hadn't had any since arriving at Mount Olympus. Hebe and Herakles were soon married. 'She keeps me feeling young,' Herakles joked at their wedding ceremony.

Herakles finally met Hera for the first time since arriving at Mount Olympus. She had steadfastly avoided him up until Zeus had persuaded her to attend the wedding celebrations. 'Congratulations Herakles,' Hera told him as she offered up her hand. Herakles took it and kissed the back of her hand.

Zeus was standing with her and laughed loudly. 'See Hera, Herakles bears you no grudges.' Hera stared menacingly at him. The past is the past and if we want it, we can all have a happy future together.' He then suggested with an encouraging smile. 'Why don't the two of you make up?'

'I'm willing,' offered Herakles. His bride, Hebe was by his side. She was beaming with happiness and contentment, and her wide eyes were willing her mother to capitulate, but Hera said nothing.

'Go on,' commanded Zeus. 'He is named after you, after all.'

'What?' Hera questioned, looking puzzled by the assertion.

'Hera – Kles,' emphasised Zeus 'Glory of Hera!'

'Oh!' stammered Hera. 'That had never occurred to me.'

'Me neither,' whispered Herakles to his new wife.

Some weeks later, in a special night-time ceremony Hera had consented to adopt her husband's son. Stripped of their clothing, Hera drew Herakles to her. He had his back to her and she guided him to her chest. She wrapped her arms about him in embrace. She slowly rested backward onto the cushioned bed, and Herakles slowly slid down her body and down between her legs. The ceremony was a symbolic gesture of childbirth, and now Herakles and Hera were forever joined as stepson and stepmother. In time it would become as if she would be his mother and he would be her son.

Zeus embraced his son after they had dressed. 'Come with me,' he said to Herakles and Hebe and they followed him as he walked outside closely followed by Hera.

Herakles and Hebe were clearly puzzled, much to Zeus's amusement. 'Look up,' Zeus commanded his son and daughter.

They looked up into the bright starlit night. 'What are we looking for?' Hebe asked getting impatient.

'There is a new formation within the stars, and it is named "Hebe" in honour you, for all the years that you have looked after me so well.' They looked up to see the glow of an asteroid shooting across the night sky.

'Oh, thank you daddy!' Hebe yelled as she leapt into Zeus's arms. He laughed happily as he slowly disentangled himself from his overly affectionate daughter.

Zeus turned and pointed to another region of the night sky. 'And over there is "Sagitta," or "The arrow". It is a new star cluster in honour of the arrow used by Herakles to kill the eagle during his liberation of Prometheus. And over there is "Aquila," the Eagle that I created to honour that very same eagle that your husband so skilfully killed.'

Zeus then put an arm about Herakles. 'And just look over there!' Zeus was pointing to a different star cluster. 'It is a new constellation that I have created in your honour, and so I named it, Herakles!'

Herakles was stunned into silence and Hebe came and held him tightly. He was glad that it was now dark, as the tears were blurring his eyes as they slowly trickled down his face.

***

Note: The Atlantic Ocean is named after Atlas. In ancient times it was known as the "Sea of Atlas".

Novella one - the constellation Pisces

The Greek Constellation series of novellas by Stephan De Jonghe.

The ancient Greeks identified and named Forty-Eight out of the Eighty-Eight recognised constellations. They were catalogued by a Greek astronomer Claudius Ptolemy in his publication the Al-magest around 150 CE. The origins of the mythological stories that identified the constellations predate this documentation by as much as a thousand years.

Novella one - the constellation Pisces and the story of Aphrodite and Eros, the Two Fishes.

Aphrodite is well known as the Greek goddess of love, romance, and sexuality. Aphrodite is also known to us as Venus, and the planet is named after her in her honour. This is the story of how Aphrodite came to be. Born in the ocean during a struggle between father and son, she was raised on an island. As an adult she was carried by Zeus to Mount Olympus to work and play with the gods and goddesses who resided there.

After a brief marriage to Hephaestus, she formed a steamy rela-tionship with Hephaestus's brother, Ares and they had a son they named Eros. All her life, she struggled with the unwanted, yet amorous advances of the Titan monster named, Typhon. Eventually, she and Eros had to flee Mount Olympus to escape his wrath, and they eventually became the constellation of the Two Fishes, known to us as Pisces.

This book is now also available as a Paperback

Novella two – the constellation of Capricorn

Novella two – the constellation of Capricorn and the story of Pricus the Sea-Goat.

Pricus is an old sea-goat with a problem. He is regarded as the old man of the sea. The younger generation wants desperately to abandon the old ways and leave their ocean home to live a more adventurous life on the land. The sea-goats are able to morph from sea-goats into land goats when they emerge from the surf to walk on land. They quickly learn to morph into human form, and to their delight discover that they can have much more fun exploring the plethora of opportunities that await them. In their naivety they make many mistakes, some ending in tragedy. Pricus is desperate to save the younger generation from themselves, and so must become increasingly resourceful do so, and do so in a way that his solution remains permanent. His dedication to his own kind earns him his place as the constellation of the sea-goat, known to us as Capricornus or Capricorn.

Planned launch 2026

Novella three - Saturn's moon Pandora

Novella three - Saturn's moon Pandora and the story of the first human woman.

Zeus, king of the Greek God's, commissioned his son Hephaestus to craft the first human woman. Aided by Athena, he carefully researched the perfect form and then moulded her from clay He then painted and glazed her into the perfect woman. After being fired in his kiln, she was given the breath of life by the wind god Zephyr. She was named Pandora, being the bearer of the gifts bequeathed to her by the gods and goddesses of Mount Olympus. Her main purpose for humanity was to become the role model for all future human women. Zeus then commanded that she be properly trained so that she can navigate life's complexities, but her tutors do too good a job with her, and she becomes too powerful for a normal human life. Zeus became disillusioned with her and he decided that she should be married off to a minor god, so that she'll do no harm to herself, or to others.

Pandora's story is so significant that she is honoured as Pandora, one of Saturn's moons.

This book is now available

Novella four - the constellation Taurus

Novella four - the constellation Taurus and the story of the Jupiter's moon Europa and her meeting with the white bull.

When Zeus, king and master of the gods and goddesses of Mount Olympus finds himself between wives he sets out on a desperate search for the perfect woman to marry. On a sunny field, set among spring flowers, on a stretch of land adjacent to the sea, he finds her. She is Europa, a gorgeous African princess. For Zeus, it becomes love at first sight. In his infatuation for this woman, he tries numerous times to impress her, and almost succeeds. Sadly, for Zeus, his one true love is betrothed to another, and sadly for Zeus, a daughter must do her duty. Disguised as a magnificent white bull, he tries one last desperate attempt to have her. The consequences of his quest for true love are celebrated as the constellation of the white bull, know to us as the Taurus.

Also commemorated in this story is the constellation Draco, known as Ladon the Dragon. Also featured is Laelaps as the constellation Canis Major or Greater Dog, and the Teumessian Fox as the constellation Canis Minor or Lesser Dog.

This book is now available

Novella five- the constellations Scorpio and Orion

Novella five- the constellations Scorpio and Orion and the story of the scorpion verses the hunter.

Artemis is the goddess of the forests and of the hunt. She befriends a hunter named Orion. Their friendship is slowly progressing toward a blossoming romance when Orion boasts of his ability to wantonly kill all the animals that cross his path. Artemis is dismayed. Her policy is to only kill for food, to kill for pleasure is an outrage. She feels she must sacrifice her future relationship by stopping Orion from completing his boast. She manifests a giant scorpion and sends it to attack and destroy Orion. A massive battle ensues and both are defeated, thus   preserving animal life from indiscriminate killings. To celebrate the outcome and to remind us that all life is precious, their images are cast into the heavens as the constellation *Orion* and the constellation of the Scorpion known to us as *Scorpio*.

Planned launch 2025

Novella six - the constellation Aries

Novella six - the constellation Aries and the story of Chrysoma-llos the Ram.

Born from a union between Poseidon and Theophane on a remote island that was the home of a flock of sheep. They are interrupted by shepherds during copulation, so they disguised themselves as sheep to avoid the embarrassment that Theophane might suffer if their tryst became public knowledge. Their male child is born with the ability to morph from human form into a ram. From his father, he has long golden hair, and when he becomes a ram, he has golden fleece. He has wings and the ability to fly.

He is named Chrysomallos and he is raised by his loving mother Theophane. He eventually befriends princess Helle who live in a nearby kingdom. When their lives become perilous, Chrysomallos the flying, golden fleeced Ram, comes to their rescue. His bravery is celebrated as the constellation of the Ram, know to us as *Aries*.

This book is now available.

Novella seven - the constellation of Ophiuchus

Novella seven - the constellation of Ophiuchus and the story of Asclepius the serpentius or serpent bearer.

Asclepius was the son of Apollo. When Apollo had to rescue Asclepius from his dying mother's womb, he realised that he did not know enough about medicine and surgery, and so he set about discovering as much as he could. He later taught all that he learned to his son. Next, to further his education, Apollo decided that Asclepius would learn even more from the tutor Chiron. Through him he completed his training and went on to be the foremost authority on how to manage illness and repair injuries. His wife Epione and he had five daughters and three sons, and all became involved in the practice of medical treatments. The most prominent daughter was Hygieia and the practice of hygiene is named after her.

Both Apollo and Asclepius have been forever revered as the fathers of medical treatments and their names were included in the original Hippocratic Oath, that all medical practitioners swore upon when becoming formally registered to become doctors.

His dedication to healing the sick and injured was commemorated in the night sky as the constellation *Ophiuchus*. Many people who practice in astrology believe that Ophiuchus is the unrecognised thirteenth star sign.

Also featured is the constellation of *Serpens* or "The Snake," who Asclepius witnessed bringing healing herbs to another snake who was sick, and this event started him on his discovery of benefits of medicinal herbs.

Planned launch 2026

Novella eight - the constellations of Cancer & Leo

Novella eight - the constellations of Cancer & Leo and the stories of Karkinos the giant crab, Zosma the Nemean lioness, Astron the hydra, Aquila the eagle, Sagitta the arrow, and the constellation named after Herakles the Demi-God.

The birth of Herakles was surrounded by controversy. Being the demi-god son of the King of all the gods, he found it difficult to live a routine life with his wife and children.

Herakles was persecuted by Hera for being her husband Zeus's illegitimate son, and so he was inflicted by incessant painful headaches. He was told of a remedy by the oracle in Delphi, but before he could be cured, it required him to agree to take on many incredible tasks which were assigned to him by the local king. By completing these labours, he should be able to go on to live a long and fulfilling life.

He later became immortal, and Herakles is forever remembered as a Greek Mythological hero for defeating the giant crab that became known as constellation Cancer. He also killed the man-eating lioness that became known as the constellation Leo. He slew the serpent of Lake Lerna, which is now known as the constellation Hydra. Herakles used an arrow now known as the constellation Sagitta to kill a giant eagle that became to be known as the constellation Aquila or "The Eagle".

Herakles was finally accepted at Mount Olympus and was honoured with the constellation Herakles also known as Hercules.

This book will be available in 2025

Novella nine - the constellation Gemini

Novella nine - the constellation Gemini and the story of the twins, Castor and Polydeuces.

Leucippe was desperate to become a grandmother. Fed up with her son-in-law's lack of progress, she asked Zeus for help. When Zeus arrived, he took the opportunity, disguised himself as a swan, and then he did much more than just arrange for Leda to become pregnant.

The Spartan twins grew up to become skilled horsemen, hunters, warriors, and adventurers. They embarked on many journeys together and their adventures included sailing on the Argo with Jason on his quest for the golden fleece, being hunters at the Calydonian wild boar hunt, and fighting Trojans at Troy. It was their sister Helen, who was the central reason for that protracted war.

The twins were honoured by Zeus for their bravery and commitment to each other, and he cast their image into the night sky to be forever remembered as the constellation of the Twins, which is now known as *Gemini*. Also featured in this story is the constellation The Swan or *Cygnus*.

This book is now available.

Novella ten - the constellations of Virgo & Libra

Novella ten - the constellations of Virgo & Libra and the story of the Astraea the maiden, and Themis the scales.

Astraea and Themis were both goddesses who were committed to advancing the living conditions of the humans who lived on the island of Thera. Along with other gods and goddess they believed that they'd become the role models for all future human progress advancements.

Astraea strongly believed in justice and sort punishment for those that transgressed against the common good. Her belief was that punishment was a deterrent and that the formal process of trial and conviction for those found guilty of a crime had a place in society.

Themis was more about bringing about restitution to an aggrieved person who was treated unfairly by another. He mediation skills gave rise to the belief that there was always a remedy when agreements fell apart.

However, the speed of their progress and their intentions to achieve self-determination worried Zeus. After inspecting the work and assessing all that had been achieved, he concluded that it must come to an abrupt end. And as every Greek immortal knows, when

Zeus is determined and has made up his mind, nothing stops it his decision from happening. For Astraea the decision was devastating, so she cast herself into the night sky as "the maiden", forever watching over humanity as the constellation **Virgo**.

Themis was later honoured for her balanced outlook on life and is remembered as the scales as she evenly balanced out her reasoning and decisions. She is now known to us as the constellation **Libra**.

Planned launch 2025

Novella eleven – the constellation Aquarius

Novella eleven – the constellation Aquarius and the story of Ganymede the water bearer.

Ganymede was adopted by a family of shepherds when he was found abandoned as a young child. He preferred his own company, and whilst good at caring for the sheep he was   regarded as a misfit by his adopted family.

One day, as he was tending the sheep, he was spotted by Zeus, who flying past in his eagle form. Out of curiosity Zeus landed to meet the young man and became quickly enamoured with him. Ganymede found himself attracted to the powerful God and very much wanted to be with him. Zeus easily convinced the young man to give up his shepherding life and come with him to Mount Olympus.

Ganymede became Zeus's friend and lover. He took over the role of cup bearer during important civil functions from Zeus's daughter Hebe, as she had found love and married a Greek Hero. Ganymede quickly became fascinated with aqueducts and fountains, and he was responsible for improving the water quality and availability of clean drinking water to Mount Olympus's inhabitants. His contribution is celebrated as the constellation of the "water bearer" now know to us as **Aquarius.**

Planned launch 2025

Novella twelve – the constellation of Sagittarius

Novella twelve – the constellation of Sagittarius and the story of the "Archer" Crotus.

A water Naiad nymph named Eupheme was a demi-goddess of the Hippocrene freshwater spring near Mount Helicon. She was youthful, very beautiful, and powerful. She met and had a relationship with the God Pan, a Satyr, famous for playing the pipes was the god of shepherds, flocks, rustic musicians, and improvisation. Their romance led to the birth of Crotus.

Crotus was a Satyr and grew up to be like his like his father, preferring the company of muses. Most Satyrs preferred the company of Dionysus, God of wine, revelry, and debauchery, so Crotus was unusual in this way.

The muses were providers of inspiration to artists, musicians, poets, story tellers, artisans, entertainers, and dancers. They brought out the natural talents of those they inspired, and positively encouraged them to excel by pursuing their passions and striving for perfection in their chosen art form.

Crotus was also a great hunter, and many say that he invented the hunting bow. He was more popular as a musician and his most noteworthy contribution to   performance music was the addition of rhythmic beats used to accompany the musician's musical score. He was also responsible for the introduction of a ritual applause to signify both pleasure from the performance and gratitude to the artist for their dedication to the composition and the quality of the performance. The applause was widely recognised as a significant motivator for artistic excellence.

Crotus was a mortal, and when he died, the Younger Muses petitioned Zeus to have his likeness immortalised as place in the night sky. Their petition was positively received, and, in his honour, he created the constellation of the Archer which is known to us as **Sagittarius.**

Planned launch 2026

Novella thirteen – the constellation Centaurus

Novella thirteen – the constellation Centaurus and the story of the tutor Cheiron.

Cheiron was a centaur who became the tutor to many of the legendary heroes of Greek mythology. Unlike other centaurs, Cheiron was intelligent, civilised and very kind. He was the teacher of students that included Jason, Castor, Polydeuces, Asclepius, Peleus, and Achilles and he taught them philosophy, archery, hunting, medicine, music, gymnastics, and the art of prophecy.

His life ended tragically when he was accidently struck with a poisoned arrow by his close friend, Herakles. Herakles had loosed the arrow in an attempt to ward off marauding cruel centaurs who came to cause mischief to Cheiron, but in the confusion, Cheiron stepped into the path of the arrow and was stuck. His immortality prevented his death, but the strong   poison caused him everlasting agony. He decided to surrender his immortality to Zeus so that he could pass into the underworld. He was then commemorated as the constellation of the Centaur and is known to us as **Centaurus.**

Planned launch 2025

The other Greek constellations that are yet to be featured include Andromeda, Ara, Auriga, Boötes, Cassiopeia, Cepheus, Corona Australis, Corona Borealis, Corvus, Crater, Delphinus, Equuleus, Eridanus, Lepus, Lupus, Lyra, Pegasus, Perseus, Piscis, Austrinus, Triangulum, Ursa Major, Ursa Minor, and Argo Navis (now divided into Carina, Puppis, and Vela)

Follicle Farm – A novel adventure. (Fiction)

Follicle Farm – A novel adventure. (Fiction)

Follicle Farm is a comical and imaginative insight into organisational structure and behaviour of the trillions of cells that make up the microscopic world of every living person. It reveals how cells within the human body really think and how they, mostly, work well together. Bobby is a Mitochondria, and he works as a humble Follicle Farmer. He, with millions of colleagues, are part of the amazing organisation dedicated to growing hair for the human male that they live inside of. Recently, Bobby made an important discovery when he learned how to reverse the effects of alopecia and greying hair. Now it's up to management to debate if they should use his technique.

Join Bobby as he travels the body, ably assisted by Banjo and Skip, as he meets and deals with other human cells in various systems throughout the body. Bobby quickly learns there is more to management than just servicing the body's needs. Cliques, quirks, politics, unions, and hidden agendas, all thrive in Bobby's world.

You'll share in his adventure of personal growth as he encourages other Follicle Farmers to utilises best practices in growing quality hair.

This book is now available

Your concise guide to the meaning of life.

Your concise guide to the meaning of life. (Non-Fiction)

This is a serious book designed to help people. Its main purpose is to assist you on how to gain insights on how to live a happier and more fulfilled life. It will give you, the reader, instant benefits. It is peppered with many great quotes, many of them are my own. I've combined my interest in philosophy, sociology, psychology, and history to delve into the true meaning of life. The reader will not only understand why they are here, but how to make their experience more meaningful.

My main aim is to inspire readers into taking more control of how they make decisions that positively affect their achievements, successes, happiness, and therefore their well-being. The book is a summary of concise points that are easy to learn and apply to the readers life for an immediate benefit. It includes popular relevant quotes to re-enforce the messages and teaching. I have also included personal anecdotes that give real life and meaningful examples of how the material applies to all readers.

Topics include
- an explanation the main purpose for living.
- how to improve your relationships.
- how communication works and how to make it more effective.

- understanding your needs and desires and how to improve outcomes for yourself.
- understanding what motivates other people.
- how to exceed your own expectations.
- understanding your own personal legal, moral, ethical, and value system.
- improving your control over your emotions.
- understanding the concepts of faith, fate and fairness.
- and being better prepared for the final stages of your life.

This book is now available

www.ingramcontent.com/pod-product-compliance
Lightning Source LLC
Chambersburg PA
CBHW070610120726
47909CB00004B/1156